Strange Bedfellows

A Cautionary Tale
for Times of Global Change

Words and Art

by

Kay Stoner

For More Writing and Artwork

by Kay Stoner

Visit

www.kaystoner.com

Strange Bedfellows

A Cautionary Tale
for Times of Global Change

Words and Art

by

Kay Stoner

Kay Stoner
P.O. Box 174
Bolton, MA 01740

ISBN: 978-0-6151-8819-5

For information on the author/artist and her work, and order copies of **Strange Bedfellows**, visit **www.kaystoner.com** or e-mail kay@kaystoner.com

To order fine art prints of the artwork of **Strange Bedfellows** on paper and canvas, visit **www.kaystoner.com**.

Thanks for your support!

For Laney,
who has always believed

Acknowledgments

Many thanks to those individuals, both known and anonymous, who helped to create the space where this dream came to me, over 15 years ago. Many thanks to my partner, Laney Goodman, for her constant support and faith in me (and my writing and art) over the years... not to mention her keen eye and astute comments about this remarkable tale, which have benefited my numerous drafts of this telling. Many thanks also to my intellectually enthusiastic nephew, Toby, who reminded me that this story matters, that the plot is not too terribly far-fetched (not that I had much control over it, as it came to me in a dream), and who assisted me with edits and discussion of the substantive themes, many years after I thought it was "done." Many thanks to my parents for teaching me the value of the written word. Many thanks to Stone and Zoe for encouraging me to value my visual work, as well as my words. And many thanks to the Unseen Ones of the dreamworld, who brought this story to me and made me its steward.

Chapter I

One night I had a dream...

I dreamed of a young husband and wife in their mid-30's who were privileged upper-class professionals, approaching the high points of their careers. Paul and Christina were beautiful young hopefuls, maturing into accomplished adults, poised and graceful in ways that come easiest to the well-fed, well-dressed, and well-connected.

Paul was a tall, dark, calculating man with handsome, chiseled features and wavy hair that he kept cut short to compliment his conservative designer clothing. His tastes ran to the conventional, but always with a flair of expensive, exclusive opulence. He worked for a land development company which made its vast fortunes from razing thousands upon thousands of acres of forest in remote regions of their country. The corporation made a fortune selling the raw materials that came from the forests and leasing the cleared land at cut-throat prices to ranchers for beef grazing.

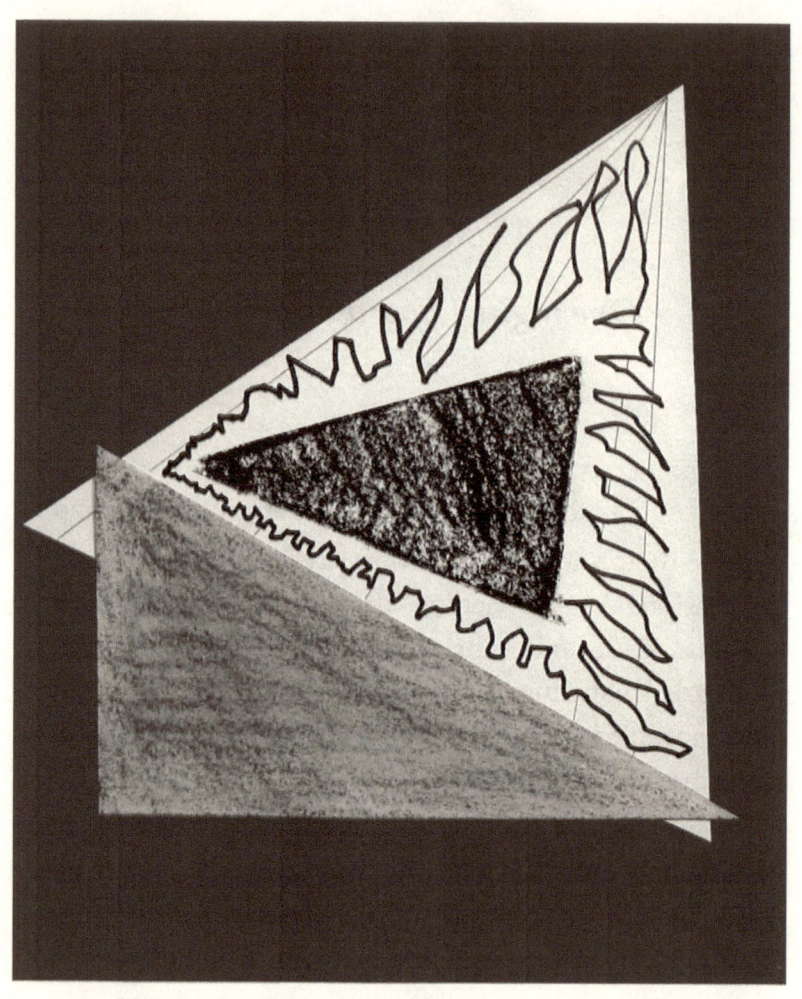

Paul

Christina

Christina was dark, as well, with long, luxurious tresses that fell over her strong shoulders, almost to her full hips. Her sense of style was less conservative than her husband's, favoring bright colors and prints, but it was no less expensive. Her gaze was as shrewd as his, and she made no attempt to mask her wits. She ran her own chic "primitive art" gallery and made a handsome living from inflating prices to tap her wealthy clientèle. She passed along little, if any, of the profits to "her" artists.

Together, the couple earned a lot, and their status reflected it. They were well-established amongst the "haves," and untroubled by the existence and experiences of the "have-nots." Their social circle consisted of some of the wealthiest and most powerful citizenry, whose favor earned them entrance to all the right parties, all the best clubs.

Their home was in a high-rise in the center of a teeming metropolis, towering above urban squalor that stretched out for miles in all directions. By day, the gray city streets seethed with life that became progressively poorer, the farther they led from the city center, till they terminated in the abject human misery of cardboard-box slums crowded up around steaming, smoking garbage dumps. By night, the brilliant glow of peacock-proud neon bathed the streets in a surreal, electrified mix of optimism, oblivion, and desperation.

With one of the most exclusive addresses in the city, nestled in the safety of privilege's embrace, their condominium was filled with only the finest furnishings, appliances, and artwork. With its deep pile carpet, immaculate white divan, matching side chairs and Ottoman, and glistening glass-and-metal bookcases and tables holding all their finest collectibles, they were surrounded with spotless, serene luxury high above the throbbing city below. At night, the wide windows of their living room showed no filth in the streets, no beggars or cripples or whores... only miles of light stretching out in every direction far below, masking pain and misery with light and action, thrilling them with the promise of easy conquest.

They lacked for nothing, and they indulged every whim with matter-of-fact entitlement. If Christina saw a piece of jewelry she liked, she bought it. If Paul found a designer suit that struck his fancy, he purchased it. If either of them discovered an expensive trinket that piqued their interest, they acquired it. When they were hungry, they ate as much as they pleased of whatever cuisine they desired. When their car ceased to be fashionable, they traded it in for another. When they spilled wine on a piece of furniture, they had the whole suite replaced. If anyone got in Paul's way at work, he used his professional influence to have them removed from his path. When Christina decided she needed more money, she adjusted her prices and secretly kept the extra profit for herself. Their lives overflowed with an uninhibited, entitled abundance which they increasingly took for granted, and all their friends affirmed their right to take as much as they chose from the world around them.

The View from Their Window

Yet for all they had, it was never enough. They were intent on acquiring even more.

Each day, they sallied forth from their high-rise condo into the world of commercial enterprise which compliantly awaited their bidding. Each day, both Paul and Christina spent long hours at their jobs—he, behind a desk or in board rooms, she, walking clients through her gallery, showing what style and magic could be had from indigenous imagination and traditions, or meeting with artists anxiously seeking a venue for their work. Late in the evening, they headed home for drinks and dinner. Some nights, they dined on takeout in front of the television, work papers spread about them on the floor. Other nights, they donned their finest evening wear and attended posh, paparazzi-spangled social affairs with politically connected business associates and the pillars of the community they called friends. The only sign of limitation in their lives was that they had no driver, yet, and their car was a mid-sized (albeit, luxury) sedan. But soon enough, they had every confidence, their Mercedes would be replaced by a town car—like those of the silver-haired lords and ladies of the city—and a hired man, not Paul, would chauffeur them to the fêtes.

In return for the intense ardor of their daily lives and their devotion to keeping up appearances, they were richly rewarded with social and professional advancement. Mastery of their universe was well worth every 18-hour workday, followed by long evenings of paperwork or parties. Like others in their social milieu, they paid little attention to politics, unless it directly affected their social or professional positions, and they paid even less attention to the implications (moral or social) of their work. They were eagerly and intentionally devoid of any ethically responsible impulse, and they considered social consciousness the bastard child of the morally invasive Church. Their only profession of faith was that those who had less than they, had been somehow remiss in their socio-economic or karmic obligations, to live such meager lives. Those who had less, they believed, were either lazy or stupid and had earned their low station in life. Everyone, they believed, got exactly what they deserved.

Paul and Christina had it all, and they assumed they deserved no less.

Chapter II

But one day, things changed. Their maid, Maria, arrived in the morning at her regular time to clean their condo. After waxing the black-and-white tile dining room floor, dusting the glass shelves and tabletops, rearranging cushions on the couch, love seat, and side chairs, vacuuming their brilliant white pile carpets, polishing their heavy, ornate silverware, and washing windows, she headed into the bedroom. She collected stray piles of dirty clothes to launder or dry-clean, rearranged scattered items on the dressers, and turned to the bed to straighten it.

But when she pulled down the covers, between the black satin sheets, she found the rotting corpse of an old, shriveled woman. Skin stretched tight across bones, cheeks sharp, teeth bared, pelvis and ribs angular beneath copper-colored, paper-thin hide, the body's sparse silvery hair fell from the scalp, and the stink of decay filled the room.

Maria stumbled back in shock. With a shriek, she turned and fled the apartment, barely able to close the door behind her.

Maria's Walk

When Paul and Christina arrived home later that night, they noticed nothing unusual. Engrossed in the last twelve hours of their own experiences—politics at Paul's work, and the new show Christina was opening in less than a week—they mixed their customary drinks and compared notes on their demanding workdays.

Looking up from her glass, Christina noticed the vacuum cleaner was still out, leaning in a corner of the living room. With a sniff and a resolution to give Maria a good talking-to, she replaced it in the utility closet, and went back to her husband. As she passed through the dining area, she saw the silverware had been polished, but not put away; forks, knives, and spoons lay scattered across the glass dining room table, gleaming dully under the dimmed chandelier. Christina replaced the tableware in its case, her lips pursed, adding this infraction to her mental list of reprimands for Maria. This maid had been with them for years, but lately she'd lost some of her attention to detail. Leaving lights on when she left the apartment, forgetting to unload clean clothes from the dryer, leaving the television volume turned up when she shut it off... This laxness was starting to wear on Christina's patience.

Returning to the living room, she took the second drink her husband held out to her, and sipped. As the martini burned in her throat, she scented something—rank, bitter, sickly sweet, almost unnoticeable, but not entirely.

"This is the last straw," Christina said indignantly, swallowing hard and shaking her head as Paul noticed the smell, too. "We simply *have* to find some more reliable domestic help."

Cocktails in hand, husband and wife sniffed their way through their home, checking under cupboards and behind furniture for the source of the smell. Both agreed that Maria had probably brought some dead animal with her from her run-down neighborhood... perhaps she'd left it for them out of spite. They hadn't raised her hourly wage in some time, and lately she'd been more sullen than usual. It was only out of charity, they'd kept her this long. She needed them more than they needed her. But still, her attitude had deteriorated in the past months. With mounting indignation, they made their way slowly around the apartment, until they stood in front of their bedroom.

"Honestly," Christina snorted. She threw open the door, stalked through the dressing area, and burst into the master suite. Paul followed, muttering about the "unwashed masses."

With measured pace, Paul walked the perimeter of the room, checking under the chest of drawers and behind the dressing screen for the source of the smell. He set his drink on Christina's vanity table and poked his head underneath; perhaps some food had fallen behind there and had taken weeks, even months, to go bad.

Hands on hips, Christina surveyed the room, nostrils flared. Everything appeared to be in place—except the laundry, which lay in a heap in the middle of the floor. *The smell couldn't be coming from there*, she thought. *Their dirty clothes usually smelled better than Maria's clean ones.* She could see nothing. But this room was the obvious source of the odor. Scanning the room, sipping her martini, her gaze eventually rested on the bed—a tangled mess of sheets and blankets. Incensed, she strode towards it and pulled hard at the covers.

Christina screamed. In his haste to get up, Paul smashed his head against the underside of the vanity, and stumbled woozily to his wife's side. She stood ashen and shaking beside the bed, her quivering hand clutching the edge of the sheet. When he reached her side, Paul recoiled, his stomach churning.

It was a horrible sight—the corpse of an old, old woman, hair white and sparse, falling from a bony skull, skin pulled tight back from a skeletal face, grey teeth grimacing between shriveled lips in the light from the city outside. Flat remnants of breasts lay on a sharply bony ribcage, and the abdomen was sunken between pelvic bones stabbing upwards through the parchment-like flesh. An unholy stench rose from the body, leathery and emaciated, rotting and covered with a fine, grey dust.

"Oh, God—" Paul choked back a wave of nausea. Christina stood motionless, frozen with terror. "When we get hold of that maid—" he muttered, prying the covers from his wife's hand, gingerly pulling the blankets over the body.

Beside him, his wife swooned, her hand clamped over her mouth. She reached for his arm and steadied herself, then staggered to the bathroom. She barely made it to the toilet in time. The martinis and late lunch she'd gobbled in a rush that afternoon spewed into the toilet bowl, as she heaved and heaved till there was nothing left in her stomach.

What horrible thing had they done to Maria? Christina wondered, her gut churning and her head pounding. *What could they possibly have done to deserve* **this**?

Paul's stomach heaved suddenly, and he staggered to the kitchen where he vomited violently into the sink.

If this was Maria's idea of a joke, he thought angrily, *she could find work elsewhere. Was this some kind of snake-handler's vendetta? A voodoo trick, maybe?* He thought back over the past months. *What had possessed Maria to do this to them? Was it the pay? Had one of his competitors at work paid her to do this?* He knew he had enemies—they both did—*but what monster could have put her up to such a thing?*

SOME TIME LATER, husband and wife met in the living room, their faces pale, hair and collars damp with sweat and cold water. Without a word, they tightly closed the bedroom door, and sat in stunned, confused silence, their heads racing with questions they couldn't even begin to answer.

What was happening?

How could this be?

How had this body gotten into their home?

What sick pervert had played this twisted joke on them?

In the Bedroom

The shock of finding the body froze them in place and transfixed them for hours. No matter what they tried, they couldn't shake the sight of it from their memories. The bones barely covered by dusty brown, paper-thin flesh... scrawny legs and jutting cheekbones... hair straggling across their luxurious satin pillowcases... the image of that body leapt out at them whenever their minds tried to turn to other things—work, food, routine—holding them hostage in disbelief.

Who had done this?

And why?

Who could have planned this and put it into action?

Where could someone find a body like this? How had they gotten it into their apartment?

What was the meaning of this?

What was happening?

How could this be?

How could this be?

The same sickening questions flashed through their addled minds for hours. At last, the first hint of rosy dawn tinged the smoggy sky, but still no answers arose.

And the body was still in their bed.

What to do...

What on earth could they do?

Sorely in need of sleep and dreadfully uncertain, they retrieved some blankets from the hall closet, and dozed fitfully for an hour or so—Christina on the sofa and Paul on the love seat.

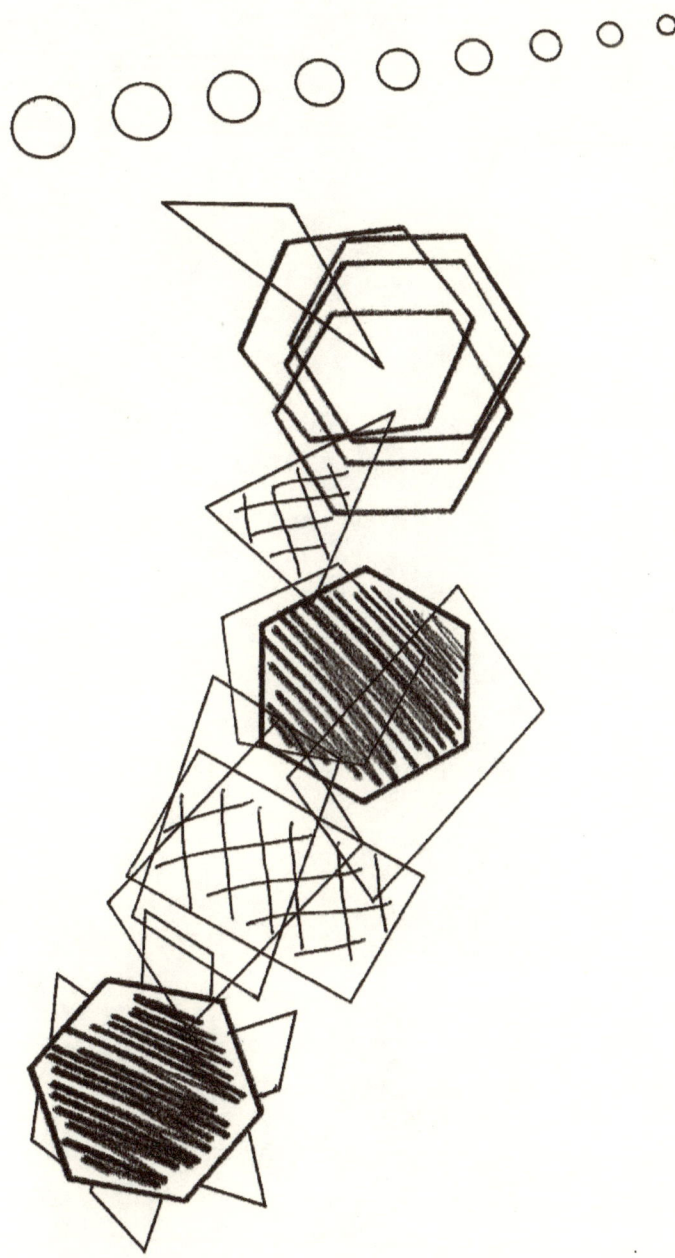

Night One

Chapter III

When they awoke, the couple leaned over and kissed each other good morning. Then they remembered the body, and pulled back from each other with a turn of their stomachs. The stink of the corpse seeped from behind their bedroom door, growing stronger, it seemed, by the minute. They needed to do something about that body. But what?

They hadn't the first idea, where to start... Just imagining touching the body made their guts heave, and the thought of dealing with dismembered body parts blinded them with nausea. The corpse didn't look heavy, but how would they move it? And to where? They weren't common criminals who knew how to handle these kinds of situations. They were fine, upright, respectable citizens who followed the rules and abided by the law. How could *they* possibly know how to handle a perverse twist of fate like this?

They couldn't, they decided. There was no way they could safely get this body out of their condo. Not at this hour. And not on one hour of sleep. They'd surely be found out by the doorman or one of their nosy neighbors. Neither of them was thinking clearly enough to explain what they were doing with the corpse of an ancient hag in their home.

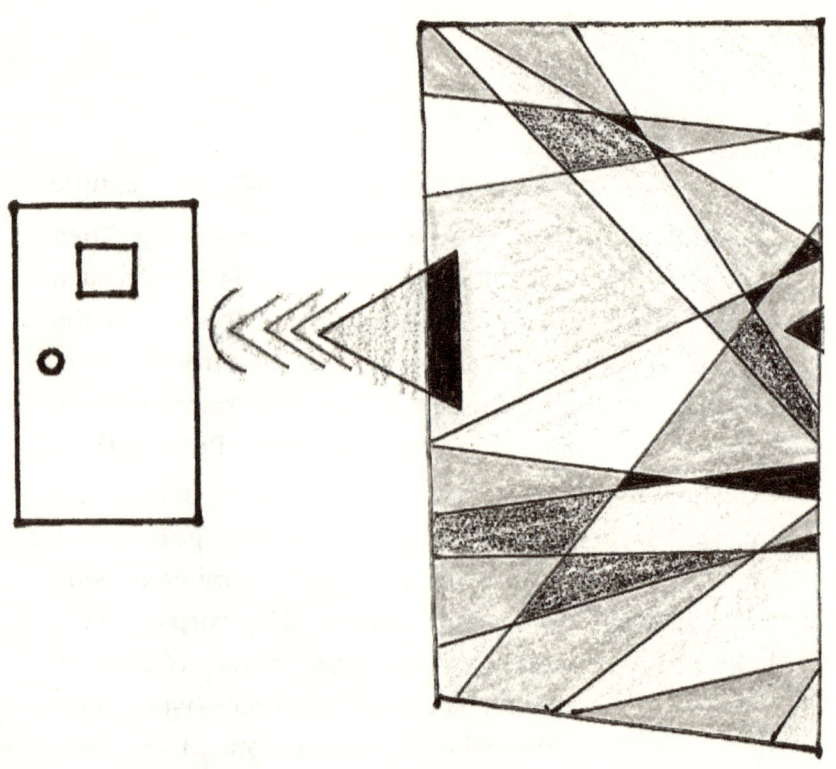

What will we do...

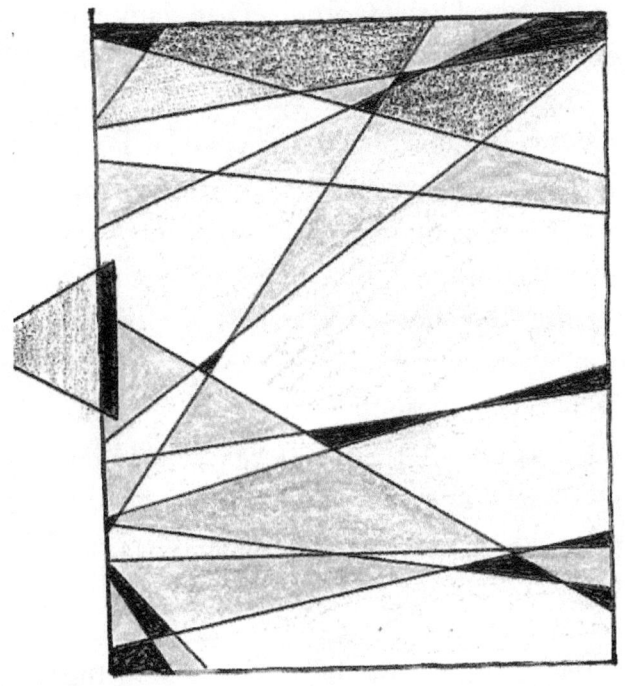

What will we do?!

Just thinking about the body in their bed made them feel unaccountably guilty, convicted by their circumstances of crimes they didn't know they had committed. And trying to figure out a way to get the body out of their home gave them the sinking sense of being afoul of the established order. That damning lack of compliance made them both more uncomfortable than either could admit. Somehow, somewhere along the line, they'd fallen out of favor with a high authority of some kind, but neither was exactly sure what they'd done, or who was intent on their punishment. Gingerly, they thought in circles around their plight, too shocked by confused guilt to directly confront the problem that grew increasingly rank behind their bedroom door.

They did know one thing for certain: having a dead body in their home would never do. People would ask questions. They'd surely be caught. Their neighbors were too nosy for them to simply sneak a rotting corpse out of their apartment. They could never explain this to them—or the police, whom the people next door would surely call. How *could* they explain it, anyway? They had no idea why or how it had gotten into their bed, in the first place. Not that any policeman or judge or reporter would believe them... If word got out about their macabre house guest, their names would be ruined by the circumstances. Paul was within inches of a promotion. Christina's gallery was just starting to get the kind of good press she needed. Both of them had worked so hard to get ahead. The scandal of being found with the unexplained remains of an old woman in their home would destroy everything they'd worked so hard and sacrificed so much to accomplish. All hell would break loose. They shuddered at the thought of the neighbors staring and pointing and having a good laugh at their expense, or running in horror from the gruesome sight of their unwelcome guest. And just when they both stood poised on the verge of greatness... The timing was *terrible*.

Suspended in the confusion of their thoughts, time slipped by, as crisis encroached farther and farther into the flow of their customarily demanding everyday lives. Paul roused himself and looked at his watch. Time was wasting. They both had full days ahead of them. For all its horror, this situation had to take the back seat to their usual responsibilities.

"I've got to get going," he said flatly, and Christina agreed, rubbing her mascara-smeared eyes.

With pronounced relief, husband and wife turned their disciplined attention away from their tainted home to the comfortingly predictable world of business-as-usual.

The Day is Waiting...

Yes, this problem would just have to wait, they told themselves as they readied for work, showering under steaming hot water and scrubbing their skin vigorously to remove the sickly smell, tip-toeing into their bedroom to collect clothing and accessories, refusing to look at their bed. They didn't have the expertise or the time to deal with this... shit. That's what they had a maid for, and Maria was due to arrive at eleven. It was her job to clean things up, so she should just do her job. Anyway, chances were, the whole thing was her idea of a sick practical joke, anyway. Let her take this piece of spoiled meat back where she'd gotten it. Husband and wife felt a little guilty for leaving the disgusting mess where it lay, but their maid was from a seedy part of town on the far edge of the city; she must have seen things like this before. She was probably used to it, in fact.

Anyway, what else could they do? Even if they had known how to dispose of an unexplained rotting corpse, there was no time for them to do it.

Pulling a cloak of defiant denial tightly around them, the couple finished their toilette and went off to work, distracted, but expecting that Maria was done with her mischief, and they'd come back to an unblemished apartment... or they'd wake up any minute and have an end to this nightmare.

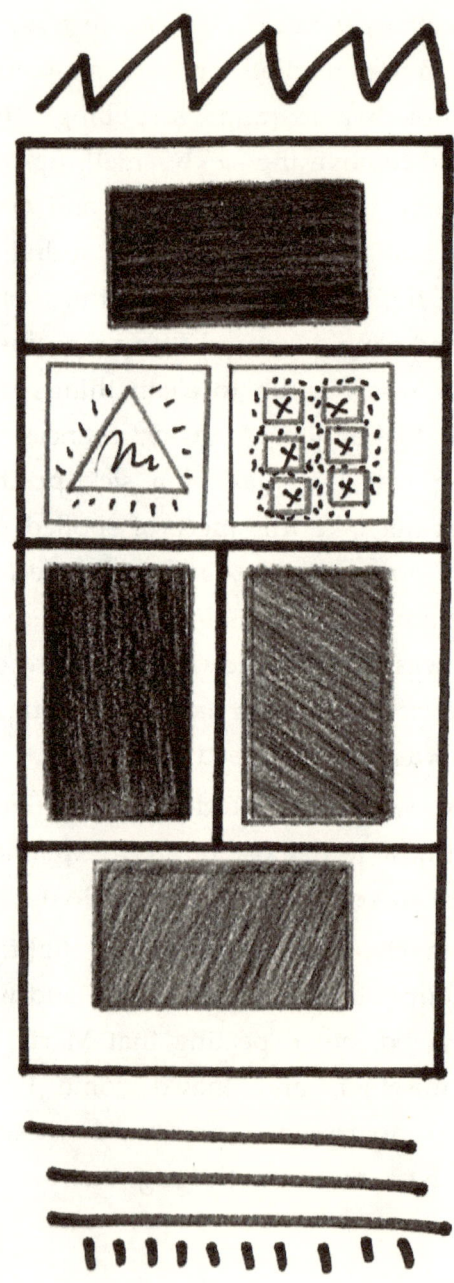

Back to Business

BUT WHEN THEY RETURNED that night, the body wasn't gone. Nor had Maria been there. The other rooms in their luxurious condo were beginning to smell, and neither of them could eat the take-out food Paul had picked up on the way home. Hoping to air the place out, they opened windows and lit some incense they'd bought in Tibet the summer before. Paul tried to watch television, while Christina tried to finish paperwork, but the smell of rotting flesh was so intrusive, neither could concentrate or relax.

They wanted to run... to hide... to check into the luxury penthouse in their favorite hotel... but they couldn't risk leaving their apartment. The neighbors might complain to the superintendent, who had a habit of just letting himself into people's condos unannounced and uninvited. They couldn't take that chance. They had to keep guard, till this problem was resolved.

Again, they spent the night on the sofa and loveseat, knowing they had to do something, but without a clue where to begin... hoping with all their might that they would wake up and find their grisly guest gone, just as quickly and as inexplicably as it had appeared.

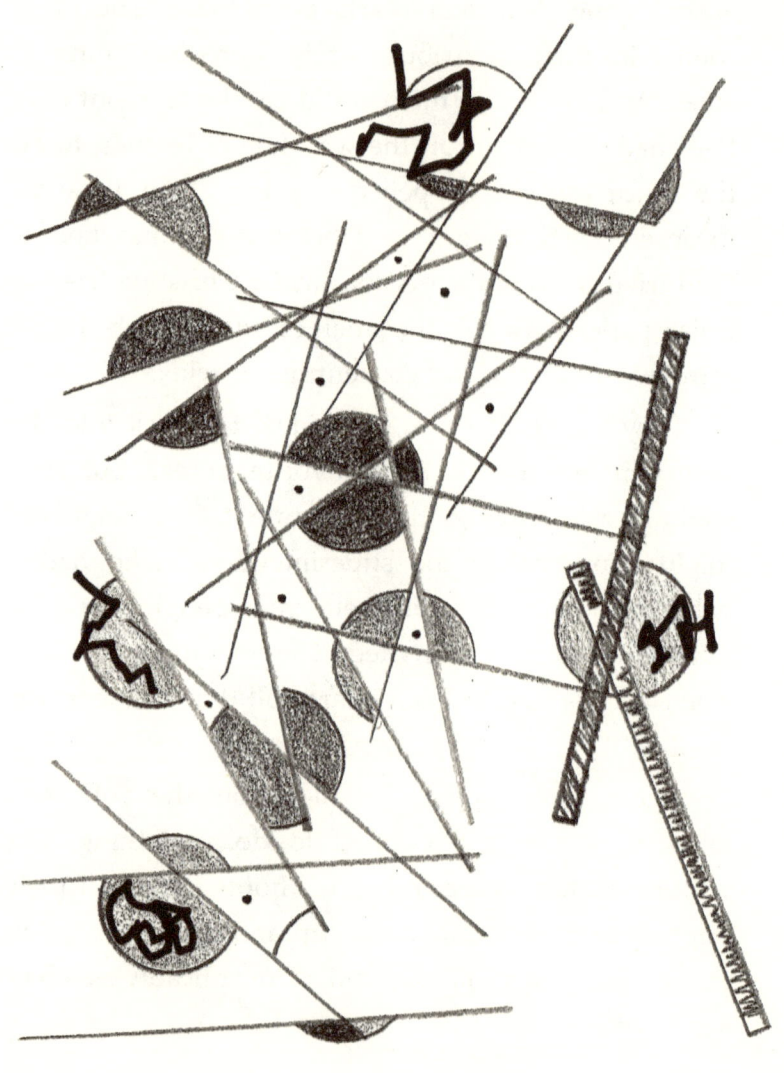

Home Again: Day Two

Chapter IV

The next morning, Christina and Paul both woke up miserable. They had stiff necks, they hadn't eaten a full meal in more than a day, their schedule was completely disrupted... and the reeking carcass was still there.

"We **have** to do something about this," Christina said as she dried off after her shower. Her towel stank of nervous sweat and the foul fumes of the corpse.

"Sure, but what?" Paul asked, swishing shaving cream from his razor in their shell-pink sink. "Who would believe our story? Two respectable, hard-working citizens come home one evening and just happen to find a rotting corpse in their bed? *That* sounds like a plausible story," he snorted sarcastically. "We'd be on the morning *and* evening news all across the country—and beyond," he harrumphed, a note of despair in his voice. "Face it, if this gets out, we're finished. *Finished.* The only thing I can think of, is moving out of the country as soon as possible."

"Oh, I don't know..." Christina said, as she stepped into her business suit in the dressing anteroom. They'd pulled the door to the master suite shut tight, but the reek of decay still seeped under the dressing room door; all her clothes were tainted. "I'm not convinced this is hopeless," she insisted, spraying a heavy cloud of perfume in the air and stepping into it. "There *has* to be a way to get out of this mess. Somewhere, **someone** must know how to help us."

Lost in thought, they left the apartment and firmly turned the key in the lock. Down the hall, they heard a door open softly and quickly turned—but not before one of their neighbors ducked out of sight. Setting their jaws and squaring their shoulders, they went off to an interminable day at work.

Paul and Christina almost didn't come home that night. They stayed at work as long as they could, burying themselves in work, numbing their minds with agendas and business commitments. But they had to go home sometime. And when they did, they were met in the hall by a small crowd. It was the neighbors, asking about "that awful smell." It had gotten worse over the course of the day and was now clearly detectable from the hall.

"What stinks?" asked the young man who lived with his rich girlfriend two doors down. "It's disgusting!"

"It's been here since the day before yesterday," the old woman who lived across the corridor said with a knowing sniff. "It's revolting! When is it going away?"

"Yes, what's going on in there?" asked the middle-aged couple who had the biggest condo in the building at the other end of the hall.

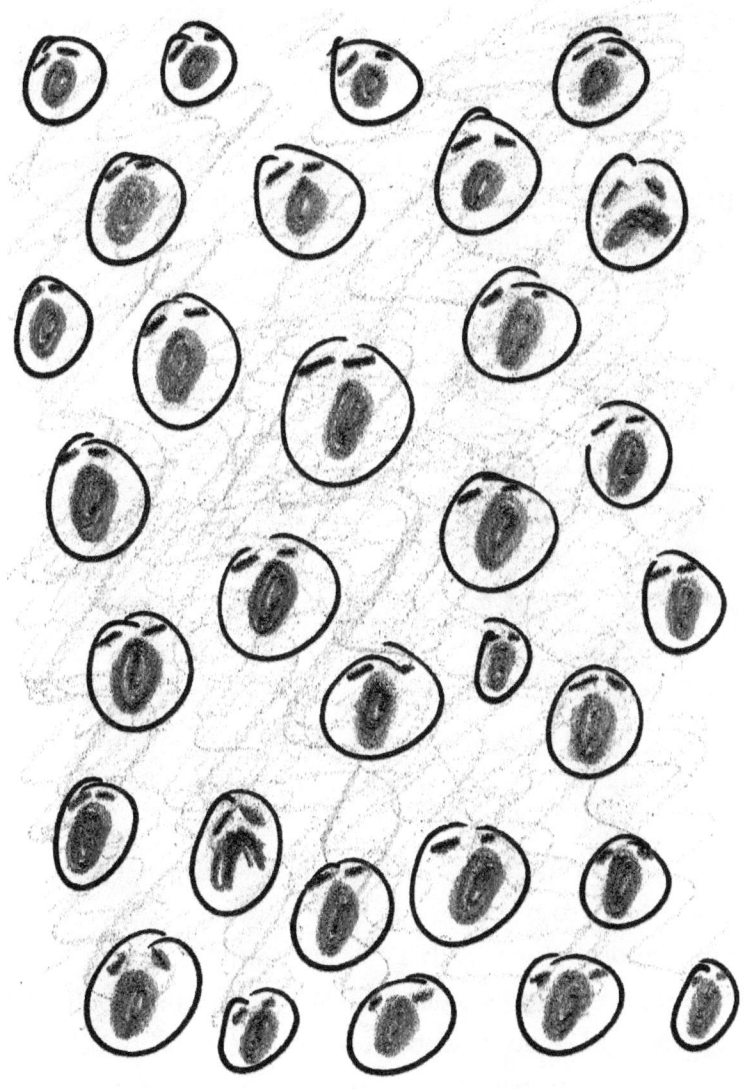

Neighbors

Paul and Christina smiled wanly, making lame, cryptic excuses about the smell coming from a piece of primitive artwork Christina had brought home from her gallery.

The neighbors didn't care what it was. They protested and demanded to know when it would be out of the building. *It really was intolerable.*

The besieged couple had to physically push the crowd back, to reach their apartment. Ducking in quickly with promises to take care of the problem soon, they locked the door tightly behind them. Voices rose on the other side, as their neighbors called after them with dire warnings about notifying the building superintendent. Or the police. They both shuddered and headed for the bar to mix themselves strong drinks.

The couple wished with all their hearts that the whole thing were just over. They knew no one they could talk to... no one who could be trusted with their secret... no one who could suggest any course of action that would be discrete and thorough. All their friends kept as far from scandal as they could, and they didn't dare involve them in this embarrassing mess. All their business associates steered clear of the underbelly of society and would disown them, if they found out what had happened. No matter how innocent they were of any suspected crime, even the appearance of impropriety would mean the end of them and their now-precarious way of life—all their hard work, their ambition, their well-earned place in the world... it would all be for nothing.

Why had this happened to them? Surely, there was some mistake.

If only the corpse would disappear as mysteriously and as suddenly as it had come.

They peeked through their bedroom door, and their stomachs heaved as a wall of stench slammed into them. The carcass was still in their bed. Paul and Christina spent another uneasy night in their living room, lost in thought, thinking of days when their lives were so much simpler... hoping against hope that their lives would soon return to normal.

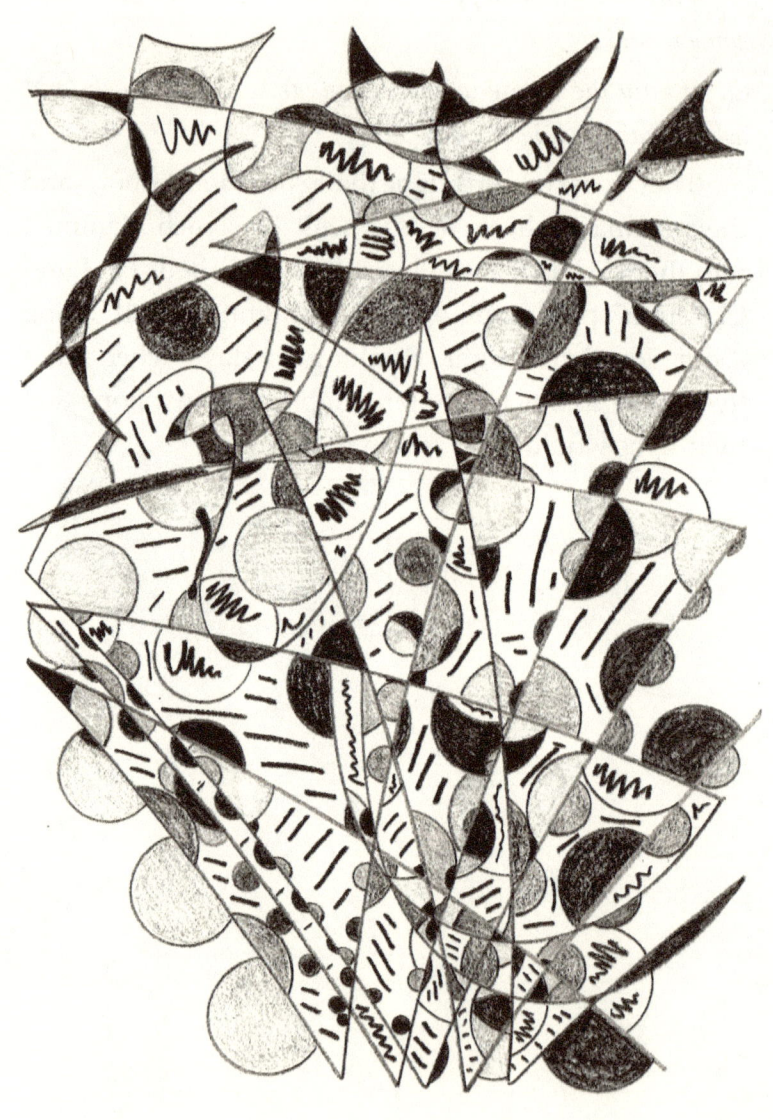

Night in the Apartment

THE NEXT MORNING, they said nothing to each other, barely kissed good-bye, and were off to work in a haze of confusion and dread. They said nothing about running away, but both of them secretly considered it. They had more than enough money to buy a house in some remote village along the ocean and live comfortably for the rest of their natural lives. The more they thought about it, the better the idea sounded. But at noon, each of them separately received a call from the police. The neighbors had notified the authorities about the smell, and an officer wanted to see them.

A uniformed policeman was waiting for them at their door, surrounded by surly neighbors, all of them wanting to know what was going on.

"Talk fast and get them to leave us alone," Christina hissed out of the corner of her mouth, as they stepped off the elevator. "Make up some excuse about some new art supplies I'm sampling."

Stammering, Paul managed to put together a few coherent words attributing the smell to experimental paints.

"But your paints will be dry—or gone—or whatever you do with paints—by tomorrow..." the officer said loudly enough for all the neighbors to hear. He knew who Paul worked for, and he knew Christina was well-connected. He had real criminals to catch, instead of yuppies whose apartment smelled vile.

"Oh, yes—yes," Christina nodded.

Policia

The cop left after a few minutes of lackluster interrogation, and the couple breathed sighs of cautious relief. Their neighbors dispersed, glaring suspiciously at Paul and Christina as they slowly withdrew back into their apartments.

"Now what?" Christina said, once they were inside and the hallway was silent. Both of them were on the verge of panic. "We have to get rid of the body, but how? For more than two days, it's been with us. Whoever put it in our bed isn't taking it away. We can't wait around for someone to come to our rescue. We have to *do something*."

Donning old clothes and tying kerchiefs around their faces, they pulled on pairs of Maria's latex work gloves and wrapped the body in blankets. Choking back nausea, they rolled it out of bed and tried shoving it into the closet, hoping the smell would abate.

It didn't.

The rest of the day, they spent at home, wrapping the body in sheets and more blankets, pulling it around the apartment, stuffing it different hiding places, sniffing till their noses were sore, and wracking their brains for a real answer to this impossible question—*what to do?*

They tried spraying perfume and cologne around the condo, but that only added to the olfactory insult. The funk still lingered... it even seemed to grow worse.

Lost in Thought

There was no escaping the presence, the weight, the sickening bulk of rotting flesh that flopped around in their arms as they crammed it into this closet, forced it into that one, jammed it under the bed... behind the sofa... lugging it around the apartment in desperation. Finally, they ran out of possible hiding places and energy, and just left the body bundled in their linen closet, stinking up sheets and blankets.

They spent another miserable evening in the living room, staring out the broad picture window at the city they'd once considered their playground but now feared with the dread of unpardonable secrets.

Later that night, as the moon rose high in the sky, Christina had an idea. "Let's call Maria." By now, they didn't care whether or not she was responsible for this fiasco. They just needed a solution. And who better to ask, than Maria? She lived in a part of town known for its crime and shady characters. Even if she wasn't the source of the carcass, she—or someone she knew—would know better than they, how to get rid of it. She was from the underclass—for all they knew, the underworld. If anyone knew someone who could take this body off their hands, it was their maid.

Yes, they'd call Maria.

Hands shaking, desperate, one ear turned to the door for a return visit from the neighbors—or the police—Christina dialed Maria's number, muttering a prayer to some indeterminate deity under her breath. But when the maid heard her voice, she hung up without a word.

Christina waited a few minutes, then called her back, pleading with her breathlessly to *help them*, as soon as Maria picked up the phone. The maid stayed on the line just a moment longer this time, the sharp sounds of an old man cursing in a countryside dialect in the background.

Christina pleaded for her help. *"Maria, please... Can you help us? Do you know anything about the body? Do you know where it came from? Do you know what we can do? We're desperate and we don't blame you for the corpse being in our bed. We just need help, and you're the only person we can turn to. Please, **we need your help**..."* The words raced out with desperate humility that surprised both women on the phone.

"I don't know anything about this dirty business," Maria said coldly. "The body was just there when I got to the apartment to clean..."

"We're not saying it's your fault or that you did anything wrong. Just—" Christina paused, "Do you know where it came from? Who could have left it there?"

Maria was silent a moment. "Not **who**..." she said in a low voice as the old man talked louder at her, fussing and agitated. "... but **what**."

Snapping a command at the old man in a tongue Christina didn't recognize, Maria sounded like she closed a door, and all was silent on the maid's end of the line. Christina heard her take a deep breath and light a cigarette.

Christina paused, firmly waving off Paul's frantic, incoherent babbling about *what was happening on the other end of the line.*

Maria's breathing was slow and measured. "I've heard stories," she said tentatively, taking a long drag of her cigarette. "Tales about people who were living wrong—criminals, gangsters, men who beat their wives, women who tortured their children—and how their bad lives and evil deeds took on a physical form, haunting them until they began to live right."

"I don't understand," Christina said, pushing Paul back as he reached for the phone. Her husband left the room and picked up the other line in the dining room.

Christina's head raced with unfamiliar uncertainty. *What had Paul done? What had she done? What didn't they know?*

"But what have *we* done?" she protested incredulously.

"I'm not sure, but you must have done *something* wrong," Maria said. "I don't know what—and I don't care what—but I can't come to work for you anymore. I shouldn't even be talking to you. It might rub off on me, or something." Her voice grew distant and it sounded like she was about to hang up the phone.

Paul broke in, pleading quickly and loudly, begging Maria to help them. *Please help them.*

But Maria held firm. "I can't have anything to do with you," she said. "I have to go."

"Please, Maria—we're desperate," husband and wife begged together. "The police have been here, the neighbors are giving us trouble... We'll give you money—anything—any price—just name it... Please, we go back a long way—almost four years—we'd be indebted forever..."

Maria paused. "Well, I can't take your dirty money, and I can't help you get rid of the body myself, but do I know of somebody who can."

"Who? Who are they?" Christina asked in a rush. A sudden sense of relief flooded through her, and for the first time in days, she felt there might be a way out of this terrible predicament.

"There's an Old One," said Maria, almost whispering. "An old medicine man out in the forests, who lives deep in the heart of the jungle. He can tell you what to do. It won't be easy, or cheap," she said, "but he can help you."

"Anything—" Paul gasped. "We'll do whatever it takes to get this corpse—this *thing*—out of here."

"Get a pen and paper and write down carefully what I tell you..." Maria said.

Chapter V

The couple took down every detail Maria gave them, without question and without doubt. This was their chance, their last and best chance.

They put everything at work on hold and launched into high gear, preparing for their trip into the jungle. They sold off stocks and withdrew thousands of dollars from their accounts to pay for backwoods supplies and compensate the Old One. Paul referred all his appointments to colleagues, and Christina turned over the upcoming gallery opening to her assistants. They told no one when they planned to return. After all, if this gambit didn't work, they might not be able to. Making excuses about a dying parent, Paul reserved one of his company's planes, and the couple flew out to one of the remotest corners of the jungle to find Maria's medicine man.

It took nearly a day to make the trip in the little twin-engine plane; husband and wife held each other's hands tightly the whole flight. Once there, it took another two days to find and hire a local guide with mules and supplies, then slog through the rain forest

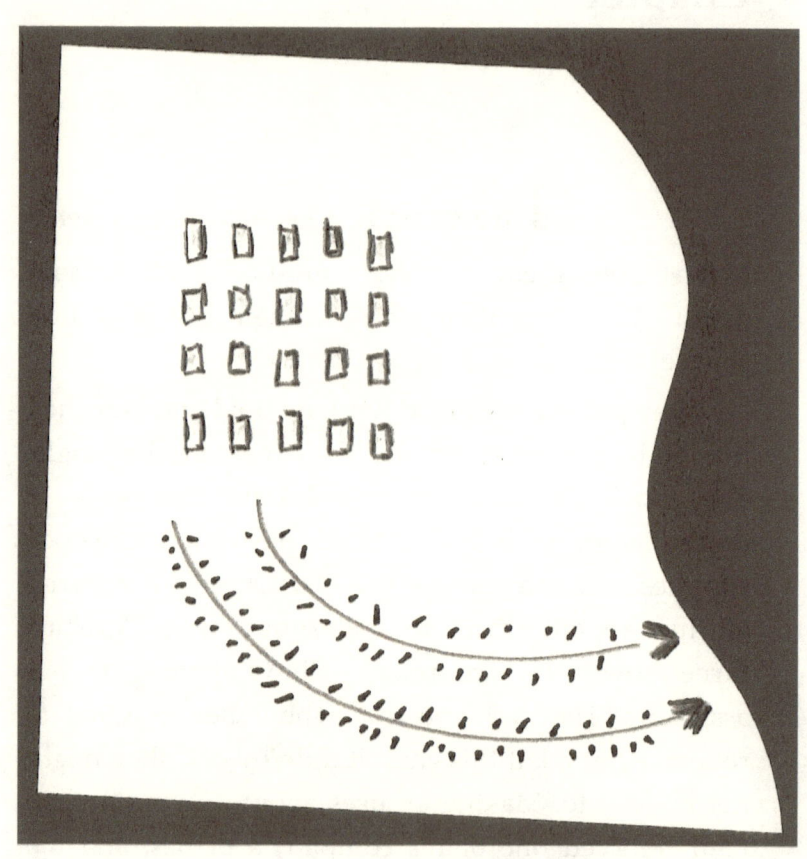

To the

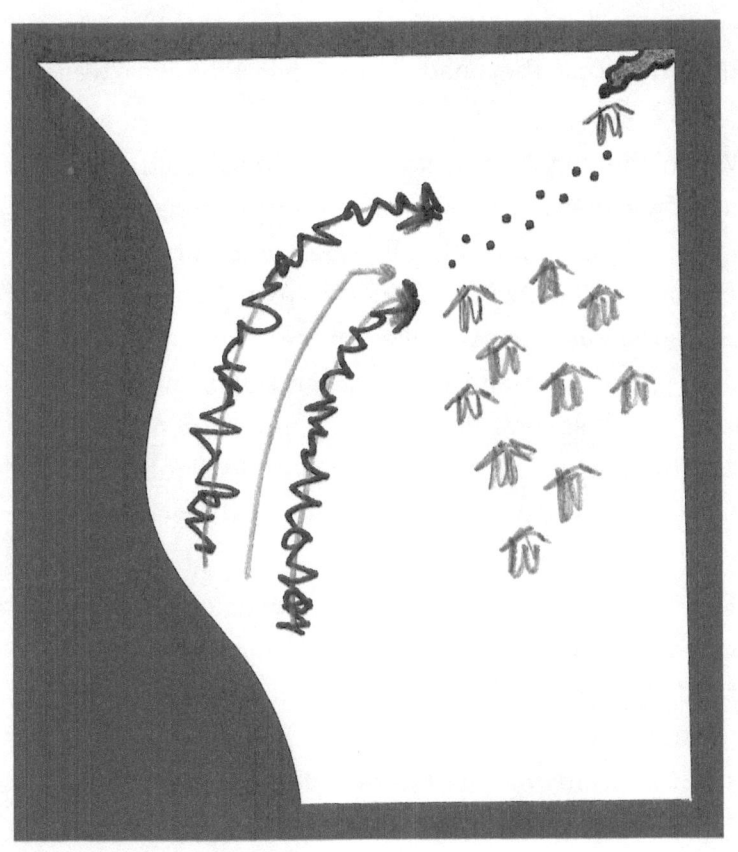

Old One

which separated them from the medicine man's village. The cries of birds and monkeys filled the air, along with startling calls from animals they didn't recognize, but which made their guide look around furtively. The couple steeled their urban nerves and pressed on, plunging deeper into the jungle, holding to the only hope they had of making right was was wrong at home.

When they arrived at the village Maria told them about, they were met by a crowd of suspicious villagers. Their guide, clearly uneasy about leading them into this isolated spot, tried to explain why they were there, as nearly-naked men, women, and children pressed menacingly around the uninvited visitors. After several moments of tense attempts to explain themselves with indigenous dialect and hand gestures, they were escorted to the medicine man's hut.

The Old One was an ancient, wizened, shaggy figure who crouched by a low, crackling fire. As they hesitantly approached, he looked up from the flames and regarded them narrowly with a baleful eye. They knelt before him and in fearful, stammering voices, said they needed his help. *He was their only chance.* They began to recount their tale of woe.

But he stopped them with a wave, saying he knew who they were and why they'd come. They should say no more. He knew what their problem was, and how to fix it.

"But it won't be easy for you to do this thing," he said matter-of-factly, looking them up and down with a mixture of disdain and pity. "And you probably won't want to bother."

"We'll do *anything*," they insisted resolutely, "Just tell us what. We'll do exactly what you tell us to."

The Old One was quiet for a long time, staring into the fire. Then he nodded, "Yes—You will."

He led them into another brush hut on the other side of the settlement; all the villagers crowded around them, pressing closer to see what these intruders were up to.

Inside the hut, the air was thick with the scent of herbs. Smoke hovered in the narrow beams of sunlight which filtered through the walls, tricking the eyes with its dance. The couple exchanged nervous glances, warily elated that they'd found their medicine man, deliberately daring to hope that he could truly help them.

Quickly and insistently, the Old One taught them ceremony for a full, intense day, teaching them an intricate ritual which would clear their misdeeds and return their spirits to normal. Paul wasn't sure he could remember anything he was being shown, and Christina was certain their lesson would take at least several days to learn, but the medicine man worked quickly, urgently, teaching them specific hand motions and words and melodic chants, intolerant of any error. He had them repeat the phrases and incantations and mirror his movements over and over, quickly, precisely, genuinely from their beleaguered hearts, until they could perform the complex rite without needing his prompting.

When the light of dawn at last tinged the skies, he sent them into the forest by themselves to perform their rituals. They were allowed to take none of the supplies they'd brought, only their medicine plants and water. Per his strict instructions, they were to precisely pronounce each word he'd taught them... using the herbs and performing the intricate motions he'd showed them with care.

"You may eat no food for three days and drink only the water you carry with you," he warned, as though to fail would mean their ruin. In their hearts, both of them were sure it would.

Into the forest Paul and Christina hiked... without a guide or food or camping supplies... without any idea what lay before them. The horror of their unwanted house guest was still vivid in their minds, and their guts churned with anxiety... but the thought of going home to that horror spurred them deeper into the jungle.

What if this didn't work?

It had to work.

They had to make it work.

This was their only chance to get their lives back.

*Yes, it **had** to work.*

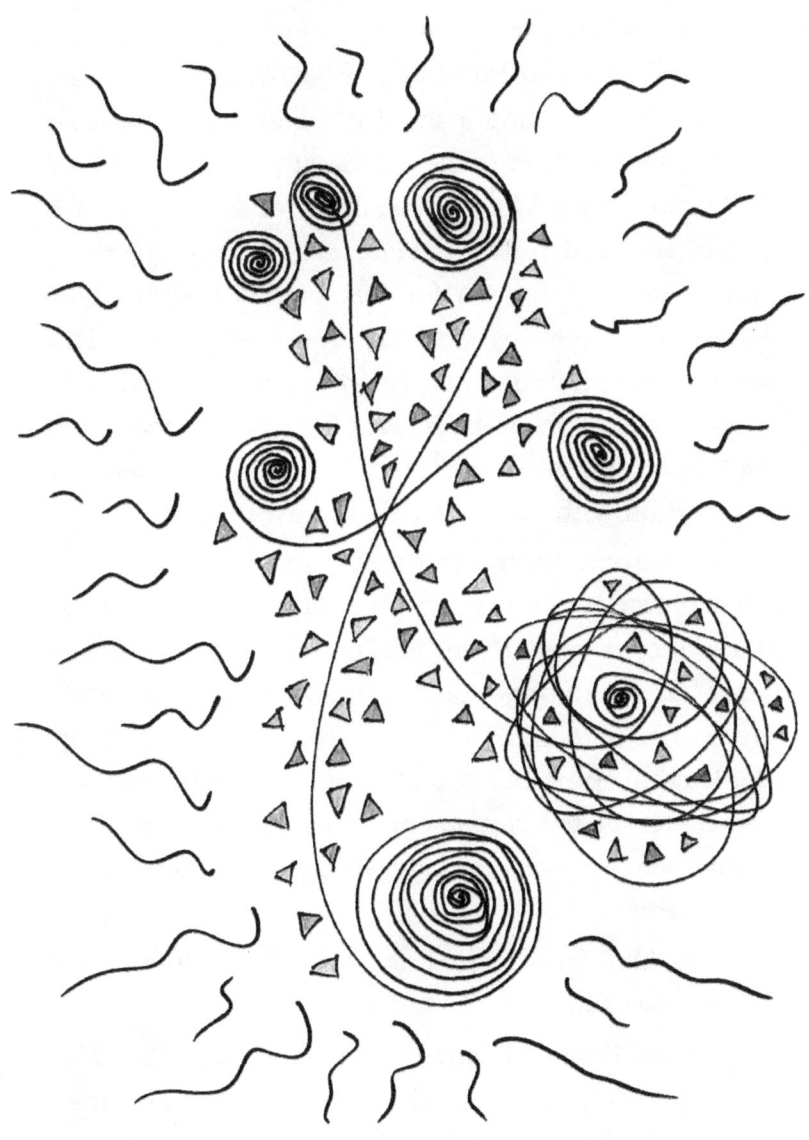

Ceremony

They found the remote, secluded clearing the medicine man had told them about, deep in the heart of the forest. Making a small fire and arranging their herbs around them, they did exactly as the Old One had told them, with painstaking attention to each detail. They didn't dare deviate one iota from the ritual he'd laid out for them for fear of failure—and who knew what fate—when they returned home. This crash course in indigenous ceremony was a small price to pay to save themselves, and they performed every motion, pronounced every word, recited every lengthy incantation with reverent, deliberate intensity.

At the end of the third day, they completed the final phase of the ritual and used up the last of the herbs they'd been given. Praying for success, but not quite daring to hope for as much, they retraced their steps back to the village. Stumbling, bumbling, depleted in spirit, mind, and body, they all but fell into the center of the settlement. Their city clothes hung from them in limp, sweaty shreds, but their spirits were lighter.

The Old One looked them up and down. "Go home," he said.

Dazed, Paul and Christina just looked at him. *That was it?* they wondered numbly through their exhaustion. They tried to offer him the money they'd brought with them, but he dismissed them with a wave.

"It's taken care of," he said simply, and the couple's hearts leaped with a faint glimmer of hope. "*But,*" he warned them before they turned away, "You must do even more. You must swear to change your work and ways, and stop wrecking the forests. You must not misuse anything that comes from the land. No, you must guard the land now, if you want things to be better for you. You must go back home and get rid of all traces of the things that led you down this path—and you know what they are. You must get rid of the trinkets from the forest you collect for fun, and not use people like you use your car or your wristwatch. You must be mindful of the life you lead and not just take whatever you like, from whomever you like, just for your own selfish pleasure. You must never again buy anything made from the precious wood logged from the forests, nor may you eat any of the beef from the cattle now grazing on clear-cut land. You must never, ever take life for granted again, and you must carefully consider everything you put into your mouths and on your bodies.

"You know what you must do," he said intently. "You always have. Now you must **do** it."

"Yes, yes," the couple agreed, bowing. "We **will** change our ways." And with their hearts a little lighter, they walked out of the jungle, met up with the company plane and flew back, apprehensive, but too tired to worry. Holding hands tightly, they slept soundly the whole flight back—for the first time in over a week.

Chapter VI

When Paul and Christina returned to their condo, it looked just as they'd left it. Furniture was still askew, sheets and blankets lay strewn across the living room floor, and piles of clothes lay about. But the body was gone. Everywhere they searched, the rotting corpse of the withered old woman was nowhere to be found. Even the stench had lifted. They nearly cried for joy.

Remembering the Old One's words, they immediately went through their apartment and removed all the artwork made from precious wood and exotic materials, all their possessions that came from the clear-cut land, the shoes and fine clothes they knew were made by poor women who barely made 50 cents a day. They didn't think of selling any of it—they just dumped it all in the trash, to make an immediate clean start. They went through their refrigerator and removed the delicacies made from endangered wildlife, and they threw out all the beef in their freezer that came from cattle grazing on clear-cut land. Then they changed the sheets on their bed, and fell into it, exhausted but relieved.

Through the following weeks, they remembered every moment of the terror they had endured. Though their condo was devoid of any incriminating objects, the horror of the corpse in their bed stayed with them. Night after night they had gruesome nightmares of the body rejoining them in their bed... or coming to life and attacking them...

Paul took a different position at work, where he scaled down "development" efforts and re-negotiated land deals with ranchers. Unlike before, he did it as fairly as humanly possible under the circumstances, much to his supervisor's chagrin. But he was too well-connected to let go, so he used his position to make right at least some of what he'd once done wrong.

Christina now devoted her days to supporting the artists whose work she showed, rather than exploiting them. Her gallery took on a new, worker-oriented (some said Socialist) look, and some of her wealthier clients took their business elsewhere. But she didn't miss them. Her relationship with her artists came first.

They went to fewer parties and took care of themselves, weighing their choices in life as they never had before. They didn't spend long hours at work, but finished up at a reasonable hour and got home in time to cook healthy dinners. They spent their newfound hours together talking and reading, not doing paperwork or watching television. They gave up their expensive dining habits, and they steered clear of everyone who tried to tempt them with the old luxurious excesses of food and drink they'd once considered so indispensable.

Every day, they looked less like their friends and associates. Where once they'd donned only the finest designer outfits without regard to where it came from or what it was made of, the clothes they now chose were made of simpler, more comfortable, renewable materials. They quit consuming exotic delicacies; the food they now ate was locally farmed. They stopped driving everywhere and started taking the bus. Every choice they made about what they bought or ate or wore had to pass the strict test of whether or not the Old One would approve. If something was created at the expense of the earth, the jungle, the land, or the people who lived where it came from, they gave it a wide berth. They parted with many old friends, but they didn't miss them. Those friends had been part of their undoing in the first place.

THEIR LIVES CONTINUED on their reformed path for many months. And as the newly conscious couple went through the daily motions of redeeming themselves, the horror gradually faded. They were healthier and happier than ever before, and in spite of the inconvenient changes they'd made, they were more comfortable and peaceful than ever. They never spoke of that horrific week, so long ago, and every day they felt less as though their world would fall in around them. Thanks to the changes they'd made, the great shadow which had hung over them, week after apprehensive week, was lifting.

A World of Different

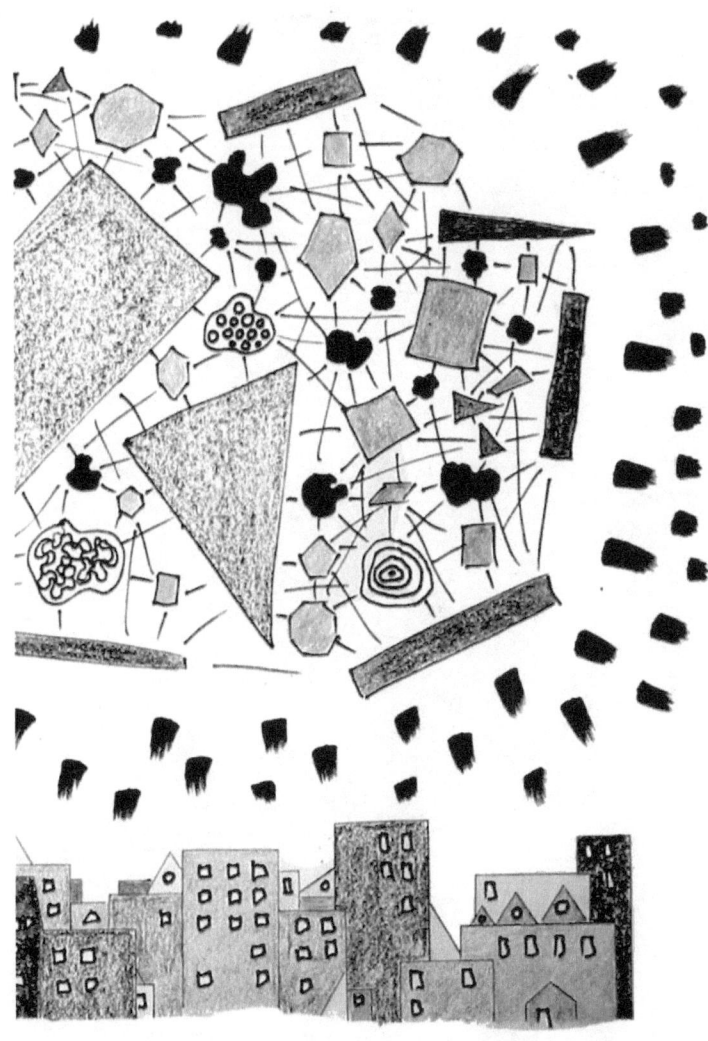

Choices Awaits

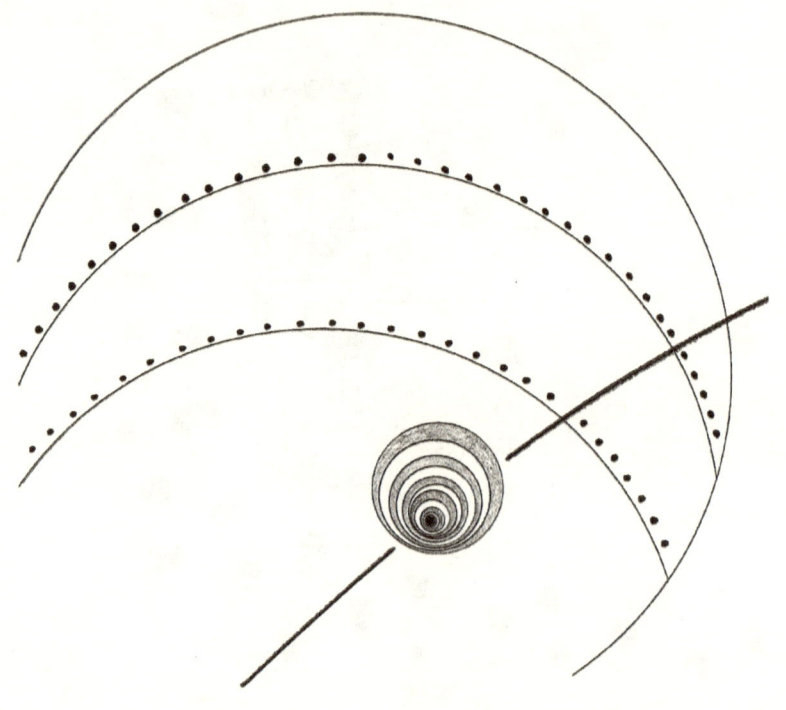

Life is So Much Simpler, Now

THEN, ONE DAY Paul came home with a little wooden sculpture he'd picked up from a street vendor near his bus stop. As soon as Christina saw it, paralyzing fear gripped her—it was made from some of the same precious wood the medicine man had specifically warned them against buying.

"You Fool! What have you done?!" she cried, shrinking away from it as though it were a poisonous snake about to strike.

Paul was mortified when he realized his mistake. At the time he'd bought it, he hadn't even suspected he was doing anything wrong. Gingerly, he set the figurine down on the coffee table, regarding it warily, looking furtively around their condo for any signs of the corpse reappearing.

Christina chewed her lip half raw, pacing back and forth across the living room floor, cursing under her breath. "You idiot! What did you think you were doing?"

"I didn't think I was doing anything!" Paul snapped defensively. "It just looked nice, is all..."

"Well, now you've done it... What do we do now? *What do we do now?*" Christina was near tears. Both of them chilled with fear of retribution.

"Maybe if we burned it, we could save ourselves..." Paul said. "Maybe we still have time."

"Yes," Christina said. "We should just get rid of it right away."

You Fool! What Have You Done?!

"Maybe since we haven't had it that long," Paul reasoned, "it won't do us in. It was an innocent mistake..."

"Yes... After all, you didn't know what you were doing. Did you?"

"Of course not!" Paul sputtered, half lying. It wasn't that he hadn't known—he just hadn't given it much thought. Buying that little statue hadn't been deliberate—just a reflex reaction to a beautiful little object he thought would look nice in their home. "In the morning I'll take it back where I got it," he said. "It's late now, and both of us are tired..."

Christina agreed. He could return it to the vendor in the morning. One night of having it in the apartment wouldn't kill them.

With that, they went to bed—but not before checking if a corpse was waiting for them between the sheets.

The next morning, they woke, still shaken from Paul's error, and he took the figurine with him to return to the vendor on his way to work. But the table and salesman were gone from their regular place, and none of the other sellers knew where the he'd had gone. While riding the bus to work, Paul looked closer at the miniature. It was just a sweet little statue of an Indian girl with a winsome smile. He really did like it. *What harm could it do?* He tucked it back into his coat pocket, nervously defiant.

That night, when he got home from work, he told his wife about the vendor being gone and his decision to keep the little statue.

"You pig-headed fool!" Christina cried. "You're going to get us both killed! Or worse. Don't you remember what happened last time?"

But something in Paul hardened at her words, and he became intractable. He wouldn't get rid of the figurine, he said. The more he thought about it, the fonder he became of that little wooden thing. *No, he would keep it.*

They fought over the figurine for half the night.

Christina berated him for going back on his word, while Paul teased her about her "hysteria," calling her overly emotional.

"We're being fools," she said, "for thinking we can just go back to how things were! We can't! Not anymore."

"You're crazy," he snorted, "to keep falling for all that black magic hoo-hah. It was a joke some sicko played on us. A scam. Some Indian woo-woo shit designed to make us miserable. Well, I won't go along with it anymore. And you're a sucker to buy into it one minute longer." Paul laughed aloud bitterly when he thought of all the changes they'd been through. *They were both adults, weren't they? This was the 20th Century, not 5000 B.C.*

"We've been had," he said bitterly, "and I'm not going to fall for any more of that mumbo jumbo crap." As he said it, Paul felt a queasiness in his gut, but he swallowed hard and forced it out of his mind. *He was a grown man. He wouldn't be bullied by a little wooden figurine he'd picked up for a couple of bucks on the street.*

Her husband's vehement words hammered through Christina's ironclad resolve, and she began to feel a little silly. *Maybe he was right, to not worry...* She took a closer look at the figurine... she had to admit, it was very pretty. *Such an expressive face on such a small piece of art... It really was remarkable craftsmanship... What a waste, to just throw it away...*

Maybe he was right, she thought, beginning to back down. *After all*, she rationalized, *it was only a little wooden statue. What harm could it do? Certainly, this little transgression wouldn't get them in too much trouble...* But before she acquiesced to Paul's intention, she insisted they get rid of it at the first sign of trouble—if there was any.

Paul agreed, belligerently indulging her paranoia this one time, though in his heart he felt a little pang of dread, as well. They placed the miniature on a high shelf in the kitchen—half hidden, but not entirely, so they could enjoy it from what seemed like a safe distance.

For weeks, each of them secretly watched every minute detail of their life, keeping an eye out for warning signs that they were in trouble again. At the first sign of danger, they agreed, they'd get rid of the little thing. They half expected it, too. Both were poised, ready to redeem themselves from their potentially disastrous transgressions at a moment's notice.

We Know What We Will Do

But nothing happened. Days passed... then weeks... then months... They kept the figurine and even placed it on prominent display in their living room. But still nothing happened. Many months had passed, since their trip to see the medicine man, and there was no more sign of aggression from any hostile mystical forces. No corpse reappeared in their bed, and the sky didn't fall.

Slowly but surely, the horror of that dreadful episode faded from memory. The exact sequence of events that had once sent them deep into the jungle got scrambled in their memory. The terror of finding that horrific cadaver, the threat of nosy neighbors and the prying of suspicious police dissipated. It was all but forgotten. Everyone—even Maria, who came back to work for them—put the unpleasant incident out of their minds and went about their daily lives without giving it much thought.

Chapter VII

More than a year passed without mishap, and one day Christina brought home a sculpture made of different parts of flora and fauna from the forest—three kinds of rare wood, the skins of snakes and frogs, feathers from colorful birds... all of them from endangered inhabitants of the jungle. The medicine man's warning forgotten, she placed it beside the little Indian girl figurine on a shelf where once many other such artifacts had stood.

Paul came home, saw the piece, and he was pleased. *What a relief*, he thought, *to be out from under that depressing dark cloud of illogical dread!*

The next day, he went out and purchased another finely crafted figure carved from precious wood, and placed it beside the other two sculptures. Week after week, husband and wife made more purchases and replaced the pieces of art they'd so frantically disposed of in their hour of weakness and fear-driven guilt.

Look, Look, They're All So Pretty

Whatever had possessed them, they thought as they restored their apartment to its former collectible glory, *to do away with so much beautiful art? Advice from some witch doctor? How silly.* They felt the old anxiety lift off them with intense relief.

The happy couple collected and collected, until their condo returned to its original state, filled with all the best and most desirable objects and artwork. Their refrigerator began to fill up again with the beef and other foods they'd been warned away from. They returned once more to their long-lost fashion boutiques, relishing the feel of the luxurious fabrics and expensive footwear they'd gone so long without. They stopped taking the bus and started driving everywhere again. What a relief it was, to be indulging in their favorite creature comforts, once more.

Old friends came back into their lives, and with them, invitations to all the best parties. The old social circle was delighted to have them back in their midst, and they forgave the once-prodigal couple for their inexplicable excursion into the social wasteland of political correctness. Paul and Christina were back now, and that's what mattered.

Opportunity Awaits

Paul was promoted to a key decision-making position at his company, which continued to clear-cut the land—even escalated their slash-and-burn practices. Thanks to him, they did more business than ever off the forests, and he was involved in every aspect of those expanding policies. Christina's gallery went back to cheating her exhibiting artists and patrons alike; business was booming better than ever. They didn't have their town car and driver, yet, but that day would come... soon.

Life as they'd once known it had resumed.

Don't You Miss

The Old Times, Tho'?

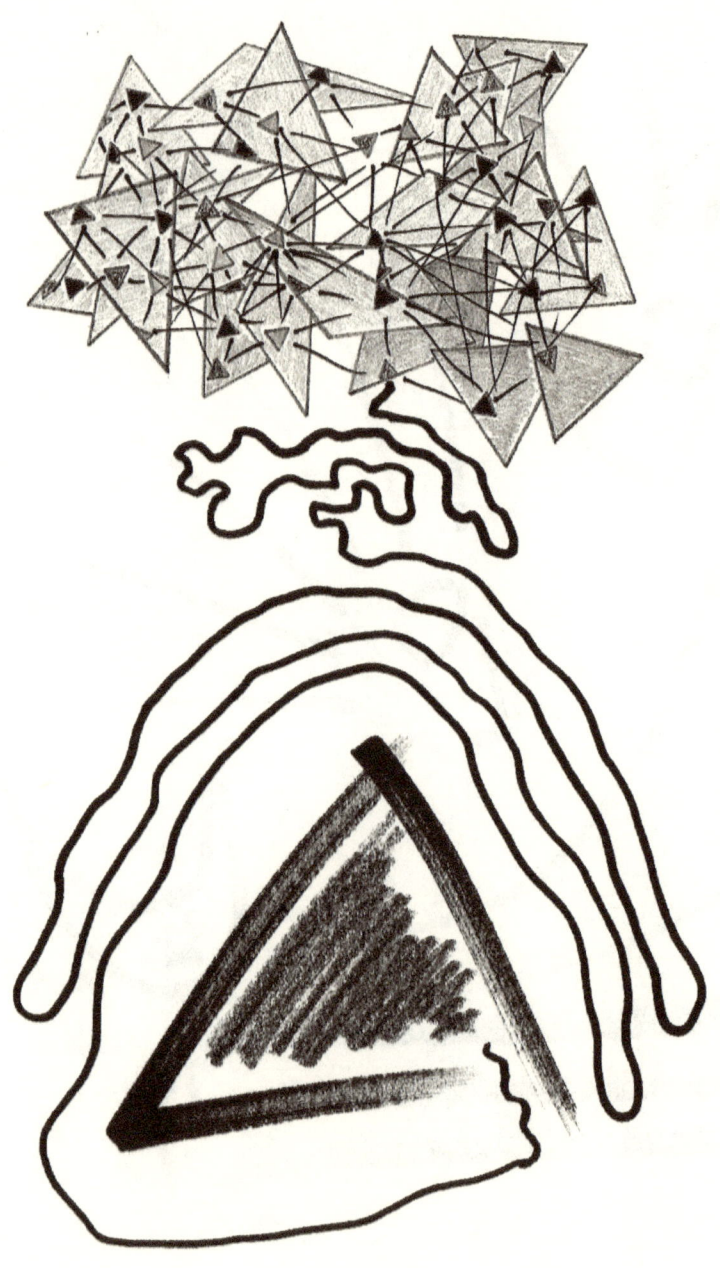

It's Good to Have You Back

Chapter VIII

One Saturday morning, Paul and Christina slept in late. They'd been out till dawn at a swank, exclusive party, and they'd both drunk too much. As Christina rolled over to get more comfortable, she felt something cold and clammy against her arm. Opening one eye, she stared directly into the face of a dead, rotting body. With a bloodcurdling shriek, she leapt out of bed.

It wasn't the same body as before—it was worse. Where the other carcass had been thin and dusty, this one was heavier-set and gooey, oozing rot and stink. The body was that of a woman, again, and just as dead as the last one. But this time the flesh was fatter, the build thicker, and its meaty frame quivered sickeningly. Full breasts hung flabby and pendulous across the swollen torso, its pale, thick arms akimbo on the bed. The ghoul's bones were not fully exposed like the alarming skeletal hag before, but her face was still intact enough to turn a blank, accusing eye on the living, breathing, silk-pajama-clad woman trembling before her.

Awakened Twice

Paul jolted awake, rolled over, and saw their gruesome new guest. Gagging at the stench, he shouted at the top of his lungs and rocketed from the bed, struggling to emerge from his hangover. Husband and wife stared at each other in horror for a moment, before Christina dashed to the bathroom to vomit. Paul was not far behind.

"What are we going to do?" Christina groaned, as she puked into the peach-colored toilet. Paul shook his head, moaning, rinsing his face and neck with cold water. At the front door, they heard knocking and the voice of one of their neighbors. In a panic, she whispered, "We'll be caught."

Paul stared dumbfounded at her, then found words. "I know," he groaned. "We're done for. The body last time wasn't nearly as rotten as this one. It didn't stink half as much."

Christina joined Paul at the sink and rinsed her face and hands. More voices of neighbors gathered at their door, shrill and incriminating and angrily demanding an explanation.

Trading anguished, anxious glances, they toweled off as well as possible then went to answer the door.

The hallway was filled with suspicious neighbors, all of them wanting to know what Paul and Christina were yelling about this early on a Saturday morning. *And what was that smell? Was it more artwork?* One older man tried to force his way into the apartment, and Paul pushed him back. It seemed like every last person who lived on the top floor was pressing in on them, craning their necks, wrinkling their noses.

Neighbors II

The building manager appeared, on his morning rounds, keys jingling on his hip, and he asked what was going on. The neighbors began to complain loudly about the noise and the smell, and the superintendent demanded to be let in.

What could they do? Christina and Paul let him in. While Paul showed him into the living room, Christina slipped into the bedroom and covered the corpse with as many blankets as she could find. The body was so far gone that the skin fell away from the bones when the blankets brushed against it. Hair was shedding from the skull and lay all over their pillows. The air hung heavy in the bedroom, sickeningly thick with rank rot. No amount of extra blankets could clear it away. She threw open the windows and dashed around the room, spraying perfume in the air. Then, closing the door tightly behind her, scattered thoughts racing through her still-intoxicated mind, she joined the two men in the living room.

Both husband and wife suppressed their panic for the twenty minutes their unwanted guest stayed. He was suspicious and made no pretenses about it. He wanted to know what the trouble was—why was his building being stunk up again—twice in less than two years? It was bad for the high rise's reputation.

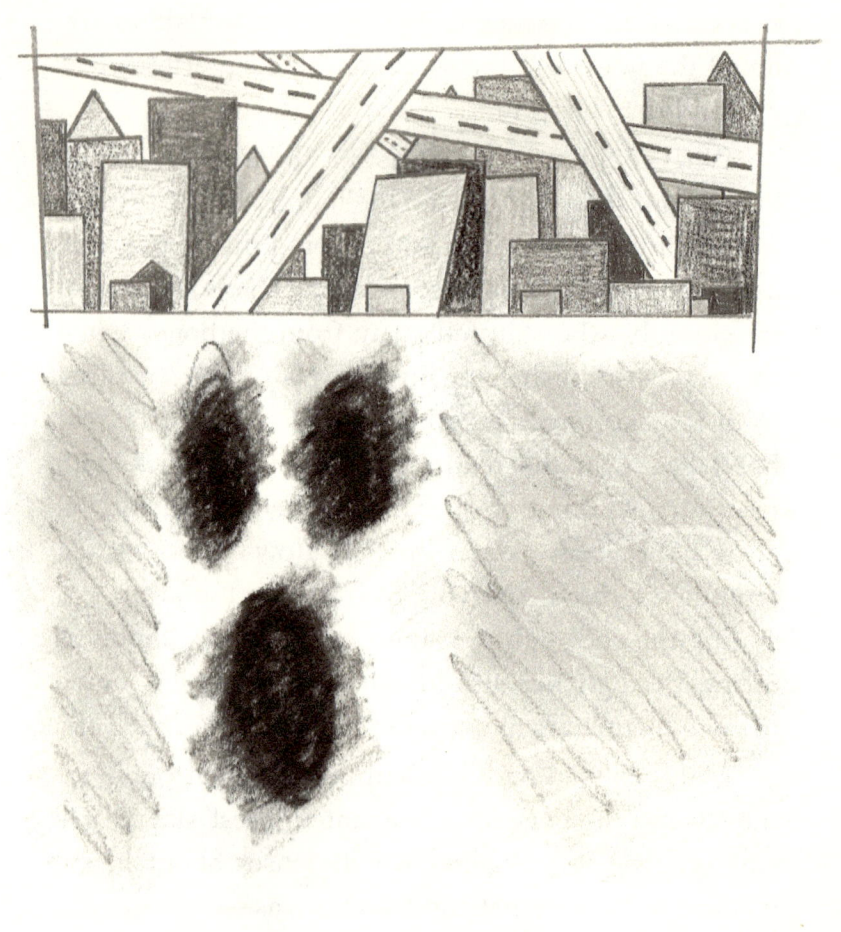

It's Back Again

Knowing he was a morning drinker, Paul offered the man a cocktail, and after two gin and tonics, he launched into tales of woe about a banker having an affair with his wife—an account punctuated by the repeated query, "What *is* *that smell?*" None of their explanations could placate him, and he grew more suspicious by the minute. He kept trying to explore the condo, but Christina headed him off with offers to freshen his drink.

Finally, senses dulled and speech slurred, he agreed to leave... but not without giving them until the end of the day to clean up their act. Paul and Christina smiled and nodded, but inwardly they trembled with dread—they had to do something. **Immediately.**

They steered the tipsy intruder towards the door and shoved him into the hall. Then they turned on each other, as the sound of their angry neighbors pumping the man for details grew increasingly audible on the other side of the door.

"It's all your fault, you idiot!" Christina hissed vehemently. "You brought home that goddamned figurine and started this whole mess up again." She mixed herself a Bloody Mary to take the edge off her guilt and hangover, both equally excruciating.

"*My* fault?!" snorted Paul. "**You** were the one who went out and bought *more* things. **That** piece there—" he arbitrarily pointed to one of many sculptures on display around them, "is what caused this mess."

For over an hour they fought, slamming down drinks and trading bitter barbs. But when they heard their neighbors murmuring and listening outside their door, they stilled their squabble and sat down to figure out a plan.

They had to get rid of the body. They had to get rid of it **now**. It couldn't wait. The corpse was too far gone, and the smell was unbearable. Their situation had been bad enough last time, but this time for sure they'd be ruined. The stakes were higher than ever—if word of this scandal got out now, Paul's career would be destroyed, just at its apex. And if Christina's clients and exhibitors heard about this, she'd never see another dollar or piece of artwork again. The disgrace would be unbearable; overnight they would be reduced to nothing. They had to do something. Quickly.

They thought of Maria, their maid. Last time she'd told them what to do, and it had worked. They called her house and told her what had happened, but as soon as she heard that another body had appeared, she hung up. They called again, but got no answer. They kept calling all morning—to no avail. Their maid had taken her phone off the hook. Waves of remorse and desperation washed over them. *Now what could they do?*

Then it hit them. *The medicine man! Of course, the medicine man!* With one phone call, Paul reserved the company lear jet for that afternoon, and by sunset, they were touching down in an airfield on the edge of the jungle where Paul's company was clearing land for cattle ranchers. The area looked different to them in the dusk, but the pilot assured them, this was the destination they'd specified.

To the Jungle

Never would they have guessed it was the same place they'd traveled to, a year before. Where once lush jungle had grown, now a flattened, smoking apocalypse was host to construction trailers and bulldozers, all of them emblazoned with the logo of Paul's employer, the land development company. The trunks of enormous trees, bare of growth and scarred with fire and blade, lay strewn around the perimeter of a muddy, stump-stubbled expanse. No calls of monkeys or birds rang out. No cries of wild creatures split the air. Only deathly silence prevailed, punctuated by the distant rumbling of heavy equipment.

They got off the plane and asked around for directions to the village, but none of the construction workers had heard of the place. They asked an Indian man sitting on a pile of felled tree trunks if he knew how they could get to the village. When he said he did, they asked if he could guide them there. They'd pay him well for his help.

"Sure," he said. "I'll take you." But he looked at them strangely and wouldn't answer any of the questions they asked about the village or its inhabitants. "We'll leave tomorrow morning," he told them. "It won't take long."

In one of the trailers belonging to Paul's company they spent a fitful night. The simple cots were hard, the facilities austere. The image of the new corpse in their bed flashed anew in front of their eyes, whenever they started to drift off to sleep, the olfactory reminder of their predicament still stinging their noses. They felt farther from their home than they could ever remember, and for them there was no rest that night.

The next morning, both husband and wife were up before sunrise. They found their guide and pressed him to leave right away. But he told them to take it easy, and instead of packing mules with food and bedrolls, like they did last time, he told them they needed no supplies. "Bring a sandwich, if you like," he shrugged. But Paul and Christina had lost their appetite.

Heading towards a break in the now-sparse treeline, the man led them down a wide swath of clear-cut land. After walking several hours, he stopped.

"Well, how much farther?" Paul asked impatiently. Around them, only stumps and smoking ashes remained of the once-dense rainforest.

"This is it," said the guide.

"But where's the village?" Christina asked.

"This is it," the man repeated. "The land was bought and cleared by some company back east, and the village has been gone for months. All the people moved to the city... or they went farther into the forest. Some of them do shitwork for the company... or they're just dead. I should know," he snorted. "I used to live here."

"But what about the medicine man?" Paul asked, looking closely at the man, trying to remember if they'd seen him when they'd last visited this now-blighted spot. He couldn't place him in his modern clothing. "Where's the Old One?"

Where is the Old One?

The guide shrugged his shoulders. "How should I know? He was old. He probably died."

Without another word, all three turned and headed back to the airstrip. Paul's mind raced with horrified dismay that he'd sealed his fate on-the-job. *"Some" company bought this land and cleared it...* **his** *company had bought the land and done the deed.* He could hardly believe his stupidity, the idiocy of the whole operation. *How could he have participated in the destruction of the very place that had saved him and Christina before? What were the GPS coordinates of this place? Why hadn't he spotted this location on the maps of land he'd approved for clearing, and put two and two together? How had he missed this? How could he have been so blind and stupid and clueless?*

Christina was too stunned to think, barely able to stumble across the stumps and charred undergrowth that jutted from the blighted land. Paul reached out to steady her, but she shoved his hand away with a numb shake of her head.

When they emerged from the end of the clear-cut swath, they headed straight for the jet. They kept their gaze locked on the ground, never daring to so much as glance at the incriminating insignia on the construction machinery idling menacingly nearby. Within the hour, husband and wife were on their way home. They don't say much during the flight, and they didn't hold hands.

Chapter IX

When they got back to their condo, barely 36 hours after they'd left, their apartment reeked so strongly they could smell it before they got out of the elevator. Walking down the hall, they saw a crowd of people gathered around their door.

"Good, you're back," said one. "We were wondering where you'd gotten to. We were about to call the superintendent or break down your door. That smell is really too much! It's even worse than last time!"

Saying what they could to placate the neighbors—this time they claimed it was some trash they'd forgotten to throw out—they let themselves into the rank apartment, and locked the door tightly behind them.

They had to do something, they told themselves in a guilty rush of resolve. *They had to get the corpse out of the building and dispose of it as soon as possible.*

Maria was no help to them, and the Old One was long gone. They were on their own.

*What to do? **What to do?!*** They couldn't remember the ritual the Old One had taught them... *Anyway, who knew if it would work in the city? What could they do with a rotting corpse? Maybe they could get rid of this...* **thing** *at one of the dumps on the edge of town...*

But it was Sunday night, and there was a sold-out championship football match going on a few blocks away. Traffic was heavier than usual, and getting out of town quickly and quietly seemed impossible.

Still, they had to do something. Their heads spun with panic and fear. *The body couldn't stay there.* They couldn't stand having it even one more night in their home.

Paul thought hard as Christina fretted.

They couldn't just carry the body out in plain view of everyone.

They couldn't dump it down the trash chute. People would hear the clunk and the crash and it wouldn't take much to figure out that the carcass in the dumpster was connected with the foulness that had emanated from their apartment for days.

They couldn't take it down in the elevator. The doorman was always on duty, and there was too much danger of running into other residents on their trip from the top floor to the ground.

They couldn't throw it out the window of the building—who knew what would happen when it hit the street below? The police would surely be summoned, and it would only be a matter of time till they heard an official knock at their door.

Then Paul remembered: At the far end of the hall was the freight elevator which went to the basement garage. No one besides the superintendent ever used it. Peeking out of the apartment, he saw and heard no neighbors in the corridor and stepped out to explore their one possible chance. Sauntering nonchalantly down the hallway, in case anyone was looking, he gauged the distance and the time it would take for them to lug their burden to the lift.

Paul reached the elevator, half-hidden in shadow, a dull red light bulb flickering overhead. As the creaking door ground open, the interior stank of leftover garbage, but when he stepped inside the rickety contraption, he saw it was large enough to hold three people. Plus, the odor might help mask the guilty evidence they were bringing into it.

Turning the hand-lever that set the lift in motion, he rode the creaking, rattletrap box to the basement, where he found the exit was on the other side of the garage from their parking space. They'd have a terrible time carrying the carcass that far... But if he brought the car closer, it might attract attention, or—worse—get picked up on the motion-sensitive surveillance video cameras positioned around the garage. But not far from the elevator door, he spotted several large, rectangular wheeled trash bins the superintendent used to move heavy refuse. If they could just get the body downstairs to the basement and move it into a bin and then roll it to their car, their grisly payload would be obscured—at least somewhat.

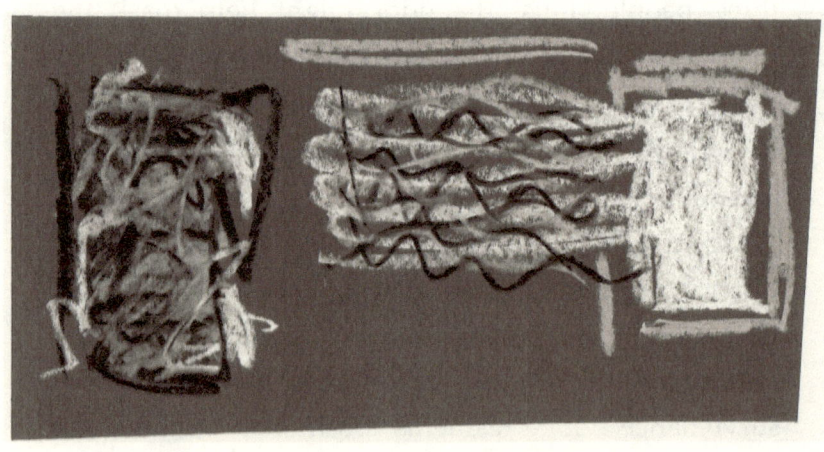

To the Elevator

Then they could stash the body in the trunk, drive to a dump at the edge of town, and be rid of this curse for good. Bodies were often found in the steaming piles of garbage there; no one would think anything of it. And certainly no one would suspect them.

Yes, now they had a plan. From the apartment—to the freight elevator—to the car—then they'd drive to the dump. And they'd be home by morning to clean up and go about their usual business. Then everything could go back to normal.

Paul returned to the apartment and explained his plan to Christina. She agreed quickly. Whatever it took to get the corpse out of their home as soon as humanly possible, she'd do it.

Desperately resolved, they collected all the garbage bags they could find. In the bedroom, they swaddled the body in their soiled bedding and wrapped it in a large garbage bag—and another—and another. Despite the layers of plastic, the smell lingered in the air, on their clothing, in their hair, nauseating them. The couple fought back the urge to vomit and kept working. Finally, they had the corpse so bundled, it looked more like an abstract statue than a body. But when they tried to move it, the cheap, thin plastic slipped through their hands, tearing easily. Frantic, they rummaged through Maria's cleaning supply closet, found more bags and wrapped more layers around the corpse.

At last, the body was fully swaddled. The first part of their task was done. Lumpy and dark, it was much heavier than it looked, a massive, ugly reminder of their pig-headed, self-centered foolishness lying in the middle of their most intimate room. The sweating, panting couple withdrew to their living room to catch their breath and steel their nerves. Waiting silently in the twilight, they prayed for night to fall over the city outside, listening intently in the gathering darkness till there was no sound on their floor... no sound but the distant rush of traffic in the streets below their building.

Guarded and vigilant, they each grabbed an end of the body and hauled it to their door. They stopped to listen for any sounds of human movement outside; there were none. Paul poked his head into the corridor. The coast was clear. They lugged their gruesome package into the hallway, closed the door tightly behind them, and headed for the freight elevator. The brilliant glare of overhead fluorescent lights both lit their way and exposed their every feature—their sweating, knit brows, their tousled hair, their guilty, anguished gazes locked on their escape route. Both husband and wife each lost their grip on the body several times, frantically clawing at the plastic to keep the burden from falling to the floor. As they struggled to keep hold of the slippery plastic, they bit back mutually panicked curses, for fear of rousing their neighbors' interest.

Just keep focused, they told themselves silently.

Just keep your mind on the job at hand.

It seemed an eternity till they made it down the hall, but at last, they pulled their burden into the freight elevator. As the doors lurched closed, they heard footsteps in the corridor. But they were on their way out of the building. *At last.*

Paul pushed the elevator control handle and they descended at a snail's pace to the garage below. The metal box that cocooned them heaved and clanked, as though the silent building were punishing them with an accusatory, deafening roughness. As they descended to street level, neither husband nor wife could look each other in the eye. They had brought this disgusting horror on themselves again. *Fools—they were both fools.* Every breath they took, no matter how shallow, reminded them of that as their noses filled with the stench of death.

With a slam, the lurching carriage landed and they both jumped with fear. As the rusty doors ground open with a groan, they steeled their nerves for what might lie ahead.

So far, so good, they told themselves silently. *So far, so good...*

Fighting back waves of nausea from their reeking task, Paul went to retrieve one of the wheeled trash bins, while Christina stood guard over their secret. Fighting back an overwhelming urge to flee, she fretted anxiously in her partner's absence, as a steady stream of varied scenarios about being discovered played in her mind flashed before her eyes... Having to answer pointed questions from someone's driver... the building manager... another tenant... or football fans just passing through the underground garage for a shortcut to or from their bus route... Dread scenes of being found out and pressed for an explanation flashed through her mind. *What would she say—or do—if they were discovered?* She didn't have the first clue. Fidgeting and muttering practiced excuses under her breath... struggling to keep her poise in the thick, sickening air... glancing furtively into the near darkness of the underground garage, Christina practiced desperate claims of innocence.

Time was wasting—time was wasting. Where was Paul? What was taking him so long?! It seemed like an eternity since he'd disappeared to fetch that damned trash bin.

Hurry! **Hurry!** she urged him silently.

Suddenly her husband appeared from around the corner, sweating and panting.

"They moved the trash bin... I found it on the other side of the garage," he muttered with a mix of frustration and relief.

Christina waved away his excuse and made room for him in the elevator, so he could help her move the cadaver. Ears sharp to the sound of approaching cars or footsteps, they struggled to lift the stubbornly leaden form from the floor of the elevator over the top of the wheeled container as quietly as they could. It was stiff and slippery in all the bags, and it took several frustrating tries—punctuated with pauses to listen and watch—before it fell with a dull thud into the bottom of the bin.

Together, Paul and Christina wheeled the corpse to the other side of the underground garage. *Get the body out of the building,* was their common thought. **Get the body out of the building.** The stiff, rusty wheels of the trash bin turned stubbornly with a loud, growling vibration that echoed through the cement-pillared garage, deafening them with consternation and fear. *They were nearly there... nearly there...*

But as they rolled closer to their parking space, they saw that their path was blocked. The walkway they were on dropped to the garage floor from a high curb; if they tried wheeling their delivery over the edge, they might lose control—and make even more noise in the process. Parked cars crowded close around their sedan, too, so even if they did get over the curb quietly, angling close to the trunk would be tricky. If they bumped the bin into any of the cars around them, their alarms would go off, and they'd be caught for sure. On video... in person by the doorman... or curious passersby.

Paul pulled out his car keys, told his wife he'd be right back, and walked briskly to the car, not daring to look around for fear of being picked out on video as a suspicious character. Again, Christina fretted about being caught—her husband was in full sight, and her ears ached with listening for any unwanted visitors. Headlights off and an eye sharp for any intruders, Paul eased quietly out of their parking spot, slowly backed up to the bin, and popped the trunk. Their strength renewed by the imminent hope of deliverance, husband and wife muscled the body from the bottom of the bin to the back of their car.

But alas! It wouldn't fit! Their trunk was too small for the corpse! Their luxury sedan, with its roomy interior, had almost no space behind the back seat for

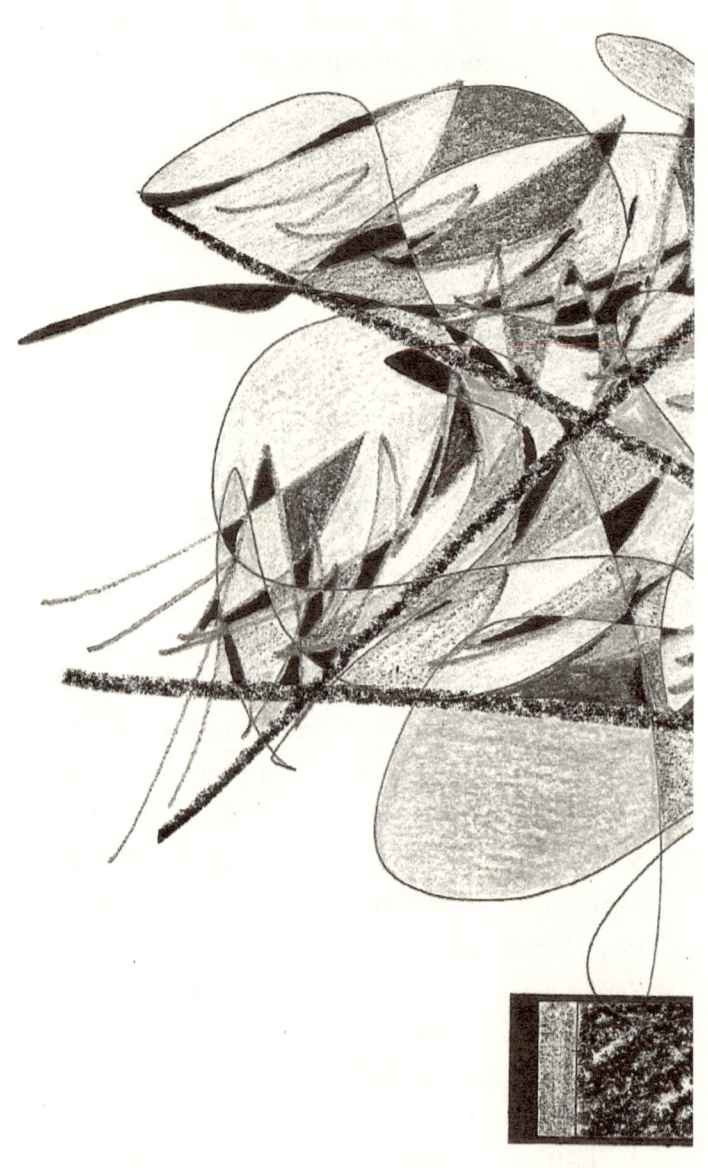

The Body

Will Not Fit

anything more than a few small satchels. Huffing and puffing, the two struggled to wedge the slippery form into a position where they could close the trunk. First head-in, then feet-in, then sideways, they heaved and grunted and sweated and cursed and pushed and glanced around with mounting terror, as the massive bundle slipped from their grip and popped out of position. No matter how they tried to arrange it, the body was too long, too bulky, and too stiff to cram into that small space.

Well, then it would have to go in the car with them, they decided. With frustrated, nervous energy, they tugged at the loosening bags and lugged their ungodly burden into the back seat, angling it so that the legs were on the floor and the head leaned against the side window behind Christina. It wasn't perfect, and it wasn't pretty. But it would do, for the few miles of driving to the dump.

Hearts pounding, they hopped in the car and pulled out of the silent garage—into heavy traffic. Around them, cars and trucks roared and moaned, and shouts of celebration filled the air. The championship football match nearby had just let out, and traffic was bumper-to-bumper. Headlights flashed and air horns of happy fans blasted, as cars and trucks snarled around the main square in front of their building. Paul inched forward through the traffic jam, making his way cautiously through the labyrinth of delirious celebration. Christina sat still and shocked beside him, the noise and activity of the street pounding at her worried mind. The body behind them reeked, and all they wanted was to get out of town.

But their building was in the center of the city, and there was no easy way to escape the throng.

Carefully, Paul inched along, but he was so disoriented, so panicked, that as he negotiated the main square, he kept missing the turn that would take them out of town. As the foul air in their car thickened, the body shifted and fell part-way out of the bags they'd wrapped around it. Christina leaned into the back and tried to fix them, but she couldn't reach directly behind her seat, and the plastic tore more with each attempt to cover up their grisly cargo. The car hit a bump, and the loosened plastic layers slipped off the decayed head and torso, exposing it to anyone who might look in their car.

Faint with fear and nausea, Paul and Christina circled the square at a snail's pace, desperate to get out somehow. Heavy traffic and jubilation and more than a little alcohol tangled the flow of cars and vans and motorcycles and buses around the square in a seething sea of brake lights, horns, indeterminate turn signals, and shouts of frustration and joy. Spotlights jubilantly strafed the skies, lighting up the night with eerie luminescence, sending alternating shadows and glare across Paul and Christina's faces. The smell coming from their sedan was so overpowering, it permeated the air beyond their own vehicle. People in cars next to them were craning their necks, wrinkling their noses, and pointing fingers, calling to one another to look at what was over there in that Mercedes... *What was that horrid smell?*

The frantically anxious couple tried to ignore them, but they couldn't. Traffic came to a complete standstill, holding the exuberant crowd in stasis, all their energy swirling, swirling, seeking an outlet or an object of interest. People were staring, and the smell of the corpse spread around them in a rank cloud of incrimination.

Husband and wife searched for a way to get out of the loop, but none opened up. They couldn't move. All around them, people were holding their noses and pointing, necks craned to see what was holding up traffic and stinking to high heaven... Paul and Christina tried to appear nonchalant, but all they could do was avoid eye contact—and that was getting harder all the time. Paul leaned on his horn to urge the traffic forward, but that only attracted more attention.

People were peering into their car... staring at their back window... pointing with looks of shocked and intoxicated curiosity... glancing back and forth from the body to the couple as though trying to place their faces... Paul gripped the wheel, struggling to steel his nerves and find an opening in the traffic, as Christina sat stock-still beside him, frozen in horrified helplessness. *They might be recognized. They might be caught.* The fetid remains in the back seat lay exposed from the waist up, and neither of them could turn to cover it up again.

Too terrified to move, speak, or even look at each other, husband and wife, beset from all sides, stared straight ahead, numb and frozen as the crowd closed in...

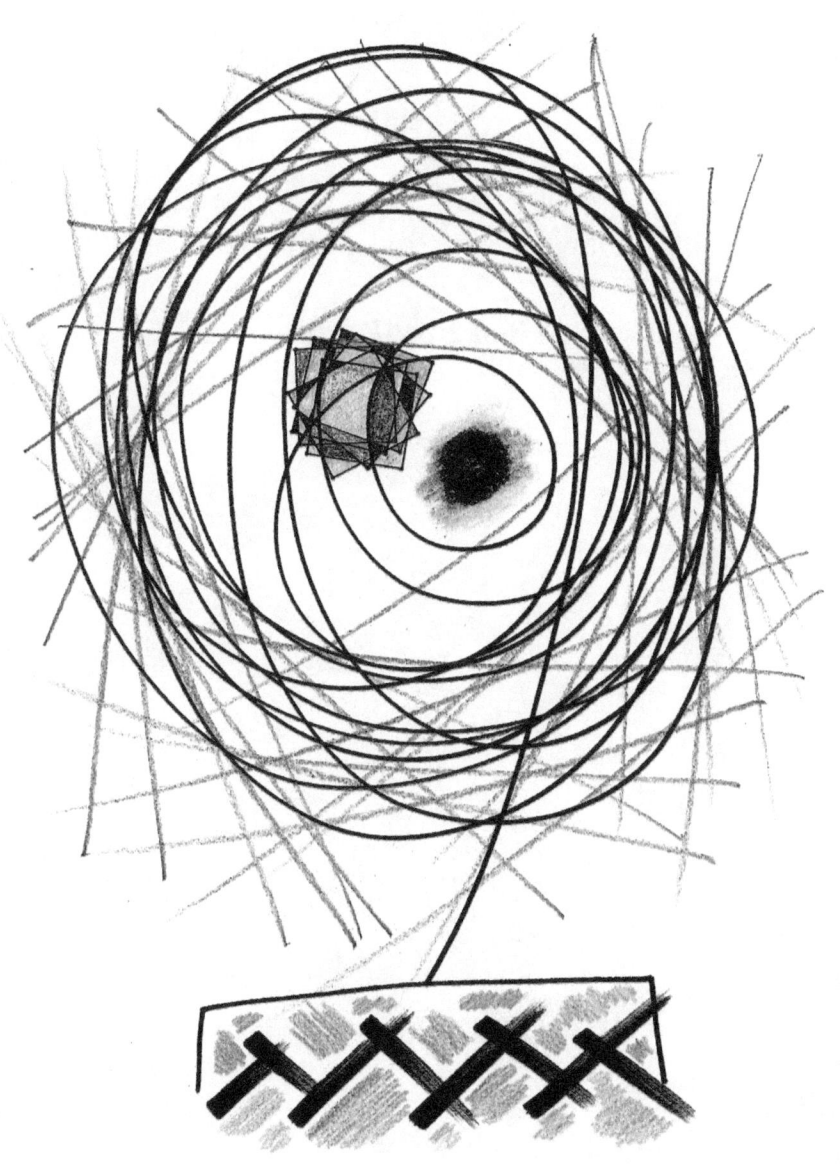

Terminus Teufelskreis

Then I woke up.

About the Author/Artist

Kay Stoner is a writer, poet, mixed media visual artist, and independent publisher who lives and works in central Massachusetts with her life partner of 17 years. She is the author of numerous essays, poetry collections, and travelogues, and she has been working with visual mixed media as a tool for personal transformation for over 20 years. For more information about Kay's writing and artwork, please visit **www.kaystoner.com**.